LONGRIDER

LONGRIDER

L. L. Foreman

GUNSMOKE

First published in the UK by Chivers

This hardback edition 2012
by AudioGO Ltd
by arrangement with
Golden West Literary Agency

ISBN 978 1 445 82387 4

British Library Cataloguing in Publication Data available.

Printed and bound in Great Britain by
MPG Books Group Limited

BELOW MOGOLLON MESA the dry heat by day bit through coat and shirt and sucked juice from the body without spilling the slightest visible trace of sweat. The sun laid an armor of shimmering brass over the rocks and sand dunes, and mesquite stunted to weird black shapes expelled a thin odor of scorch, acrid as burned pepper. Here in the desert of the Gila, where nothing warm-blooded thrived, Lew Reagan examined his dwindling chances of survival.

He gazed remotely off at the pale line of the south horizon, estimating its distance in terms of time and travel. His horse was about used up. The water hole he had paused at early in the morning had offered only stiff mud and the decaying carcass of a stray cow. In four hundred miles of trailing he had not once sighted the wagon whose wheel tracks he now followed. A blue wagon, it was said, drawn by four horses: two bays, a roan, and a chestnut, unbranded. The driver was Harby, and he had a woman with him. Harby was using his own name, and his description fitted Lew Reagan's recollection of the man. Reagan scowled at a further recollection, then brought his thoughts again to the present.

Somewhere ahead, and not too far if he were to get through alive and catch up with that blue wagon, there had to be water. The wheel tracks and hoof marks had become partly sifted over, though he judged that they were not more than a day old. A sandstorm, of the sudden and howling kind that hit this Godforsaken country, would wipe them out completely. Would wipe him out, too, likely enough. But Harby would get through in the wagon, never knowing he'd been trailed clear down from Colorado, and that would be the crowning irony. Gold was being dug in the Santa Cruz Mountains. A new strike. He guessed that was where Harby was making for—the tent and shack settlements that mushroomed overnight and gorged on the gold while they lasted. With a woman. That ran true to form. That was Harby, all right. A wonder he didn't have a whole flock of women along in carriages. What had happened to all the money he took out of Texas?

Reagan's long body cast a sharp-etched shadow on the

5

brassy glitter of the sand. He still sat straight upright in the saddle, black hat on level, its stiff brim shading his gray eyes, pale as tarnished silver against the sun-coppered hue of his skin. His air of austerity, not entirely spurious, stemmed from a deep-rooted refusal to panic. He cloaked himself in it whenever fortune deserted him, while beneath it a sense of humor, turned sardonic, made game of the situation.

His horse, a black, plodded onward, head nodding at half-mast, its once-well-groomed coat gummed with old sweat and dust. It suffered thirst, and he felt more sympathy for the animal than for himself, for it had no vote in its own fate and no prospect of possible reward. A fading prospect, but the secret jester reminded him that there were times in the past when he had fared as badly as now, on ventures undertaken for less reason than the blue wagon.

A speck disturbed the blank stillness off to the west, in the sea of sand below the black Canelo Hills, and caught Reagan's eye. He turned his head sharply and examined it at long distance, watching until he ascertained that its slow movement was not an illusion created by the dancing heat waves. It lived. It moved by its own power, on two legs. A human being.

"Afoot," Reagan murmured. "In a bad fix." He dropped his gaze to the wagon tracks. His scowl came. Time, stamina, luck, everything was shrinking on him, and he could not afford to turn aside for a mile-away pilgrim afoot on this lid of hell; he had no help to give him. "Well, damn it . . ."

The tired horse flicked an ear. It changed its course in answer to the touch of rein, keeping to the same plodding walk. Not for less than his own life would Reagan force out the last of its strength. He grudged this extra expenditure, so his greeting was harsh when he approached behind the man.

"Hey, you!"

The man on foot stumbled around, fell to his knees, and stared through red-rimmed eyes at him. He had been trudging, head bowed, in the bent-kneed, foot-dragging manner of one whose senses had lost contact with everything except a mental command to keep going. Shock brought a wary distrust struggling to his face, a face that retained a trace of youthfulness despite the ravages of thirst and exhaustion, and there was an automatic motion of his right hand toward hip.

The look and the motion held a familiar significance. Reagan hung his gaze on the sliding hand and said, "Let it go, I don't know you." The hand crept an inch farther, and he repeated, "Let it go!" A desperate man could be crazily

6

unpredictable. "Stay on your knees," he added, "and put your hands on the ground."

"The hell I will!" Slowly the kneeling man pushed up and stood with legs braced apart. "Who're you?"

"Name's Lew Reagan. What name d'you use?"

"My own. Jim Carmack."

"Where you bound?"

"Santa Cruz diggin's, if it's any your business."

Reagan's glance touched the high-heeled boots and Levi's. The reply might be true. A gold strike attracted all kinds, including cowpunchers and men on the dodge. Carmack's truculence irritated him into inquiring dryly, "Think you'll make it?"

"With water and a horse I could anyway get to Cochimi. They're cow folks down there, I hear." Carmack's eyes, tightly watchful, shifted to the canteen slung from Reagan's saddle horn. "My horse caved in yest'day. How much water you got?"

"None," Reagan said. "And my horse will cave in today if I don't find some. So take your mind off gun-hoisting me for my horse and canteen." He paused and asked, "Seen anything of a blue wagon?"

Carmack shook his head. "Only some riders, couple hours ago. Three. Came out of those black hills yonder. I flagged at 'em, but they circled by, looking the ground over. They saw me, all right. Saw the shape I'm in. Didn't mean a thing to 'em. They cut sign of something and turned south." He grimaced, then dabbed the back of his hand to his cracked lips. "Dog eat dog!"

"Guess you're hungry. Can't help you there, either. Not sure I would. Be a waste, and I doubt you'd be grateful."

"Grateful? What's that?" Carmack husked a derisive laugh. "Nobody does anything for anybody without there's a profit." He shoved back his hat and scratched his plastered sandy hair violently, nails digging at the scalp, and stared southward. "I've done well to stay alive this far, and nobody to thank but myself. If I can't get anything out of you—and I've sure got nothing you need—you might's well ride on."

Reagan swung down off the black. Because of long legs he topped Carmack by a good inch, and Carmack then surveyed with a stir of interest the cloth pants and low-cut boots, the broad gun belt visible under the unbuttoned coat, the linen shirt and loose string tie. Reagan's long-fingered and flexible hands, though muscular, were not those of a working cowpuncher; they were not calloused and broken-nailed.

7

Yet he had the face of what Mexicans called *un hombre del campo*, lined and darkly weathered, with hard mouth, strong nose, and scars of past brawls. Carmack narrowed his eyes.

Reagan unlaced the cinch, lifted off the saddle, and inspected his horse for signs of sores. He shook out the saddle blanket, aired it, folded and replaced it, and laced the saddle back on. Lastly, he put both hands to the small of his back and, grunting softly, kneaded the ache that was there, the reminder that he had passed the unlimited resilience of his youth.

"I'll be walking a while," he told Carmack, "to save the horse." Walking would help take out the ache. "You can hang onto a stirrup strap and do the same. There's a wagon somewhere ahead. It's got a water barrel, for sure. Those riders you saw, they won't be without canteens."

"They had 'em."

"The sun's getting hotter. They might hunt shade. We just might catch up and drop in, if we don't come up on the wagon first."

"Slim chance," Carmack said. "Like betting it'll rain."

"It is," Reagan agreed. "You can try it or fry here, I don't care which." He caught up the reins, angry at having turned a mile off the trail of the wagon for a broken-down drifter. "And if you cave in on the way, I leave you."

"That's understood. Each man for himself. And if *you*—"

"I won't."

Dispirited by thirst, the horse had to be urged on by constant tugging of the bridle, a labor that rasped Reagan's patience as the sun reached its zenith of suffocating heat and still the burned-out sand flats stretched emptily as far as the eye could see. On the west a smear of saffron soiled the blue, gradually expanding, deepening to sullen red at its base. Reagan gave the high wind two hours at most to come roaring overhead. The ground wind would follow it within minutes.

The Canelo Hills fell behind, and the loss of their shelter left the two trudging men exposed to the coming sandstorm, but in the near distance eastward a series of rock ridges offered a chance. The wagon tracks bent toward a break in the ridges, which surprised Reagan, for it seemed to mean that Harby must have become aware of the approaching storm hours ago when he passed this way, before the saffron cloud was visible. The fresher tracks of the three horseback riders, which had trailed along in those of the wagon, showed where the trio had halted, then ridden on toward a break

8

farther south. They probably were better acquainted with the country than Harby was, and knew where to find the best shelter. Curious, their circling out from the Canelo Hills, their callous ignoring of Carmack's waving to them for help, and their following after the wagon only to abandon its trail here. Or had they elected to skirt around ahead of the wagon, intending to lie in wait for it? Robbery? Hardy was probably carrying a good deal of money. Reagan tugged impatiently at the bridle of the sluggish horse, half minded to leave it and Carmack behind. If he could help it, nobody was going to beat his time in putting Harby at gun point.

He swung a glance around at Carmack, wondering how much longer he could last. The younger man, hanging doggedly onto the stirrup strap, was bumping against the saddle skirt like a drunk. His boots were worn out and broken, a torture to blistered feet. Part of one sole flapped open, showing blood-blackened toes thrusting through the shreds of a sock. He hadn't yet complained, hadn't spoken a word since they started, but he did now, returning a hard grin to Reagan's considering glance.

"Still with you, Mr. Reagan!"

"You might've been better off where you were," Reagan said. "Look there to the west."

"Think I'm blind?"

They toiled through the break in the ridge, a fourth of the sky darkened behind them, but the wagon was not in sight. Its tracks angled the hollow to the next ridge and crossed at its lowest point. Harby had gathered a suspicion, perhaps, that southward a trap waited for him, and sought to avoid it by driving well in among the ridges before resuming his course. Harby's perceptions were sharp and he had a bag of tricks. If those riders did waylay him, they'd have a wildcat by the tail.

"Why don't we hole up here and dig in?" Carmack asked. "She'll be a howler when she hits."

"See any water around here?"

"No, but—"

"Then shut up or drop out." Reagan tramped on over the low ridge, leading the horse, Carmack bumping along.

The third ridge was a high one, crowned with jutting layers of rimrock, and this had forced the wagon to work north, wheels grinding deeply into the sand and loose gravel, until it found a passable break. Getting through had evidently cost Harby time and trouble, for the ground there was all scarred up. Reagan was thinking that Harby couldn't be so

9

very far ahead now, when the sound of a shot cut off his conjecture and brought Carmack's head up.

Blocked by the ridge, the sound was muted to a pop, seemingly far off, yet distinct, unmistakably a gunshot. Before its small echoes died, a flurry of popping broke out like the stammering sputter of a jumping firecracker dropped in a pit. A horse raised a wavering squeal. As if in tardy retort, a rifle pitched its high snarl against the gunfire. Harby was hot with a rifle, Reagan recalled; faster and a lot more accurate than with a handgun, and like a Cheyenne warrior with a short-bow he could hit three times at one quick eye-peek. Why only the single shot? The next rifle shot came seconds later, as belated as the first. Harby was in trouble.

Reagan slapped the black heavily with the flat of his hand and vaulted into the saddle, cavalry quick-mount style. He snapped at Carmack, "Let go!" But Carmack switched his grip to the saddle horn; the set of his face expressed a reckless curiosity plus a flair for violence.

The black, startled out of its semi-coma, found strength to scramble up the slanted floor of the slope at a clumsy gallop. Carmack kept pace with floundering leaps, gripping the horn and taking a booting from Reagan's regardless spurring. The break was crooked, narrowing on the last rise. Here Harby had rolled rocks out of the way of the wagon, after evidently trying to back his team out. He hadn't had space to turn. Reading the signs in passing, Reagan judged that Harby had used little expertness in his attempt at backing the team, and no foresight in driving into the break without first scouting it on foot. Something had robbed him of the careful deliberation that had once guided his every action.

They topped the narrow rise, and Reagan checked the black, for the break widened abruptly and ended in a downsweep of shale bank too steep for the animal's uncertain legs. The blue wagon had gone on down without mishap, holding to an angle that slowed it from rolling onto the team, and made it halfway to the floor of the hollow. It was a stoutly built spring wagon fitted with a bowed top of white canvas, and although the bed of it was awkwardly high because of large wheels and raised axles it was probably not too bone-shakingly uncomfortable to travel in where there were roads.

It stood tilted, at halt. The off leader, one of the two bays, lay kicking in a tangle of harness, which the three remaining horses of the team jostled nervously together, lines loose, nobody on the box to steady them. But that was no mishap,

10

no fault of the absent driver. Three riders below closed in and jogged confidently up the slope.

Carmack said, "Same three who passed me by. Who's in the wagon?"

"Feller I used to know," Reagan answered, for the moment forgetting the woman who was said to be with Harby. "He ought to shoot about now. Guess he's leading 'em on."

The rifle cracked from the wagon. One of the riders clapped a hand to his neck, took it away and looked at it, and wiped it on the sleeve of his green silk shirt. He and his two companions reined in and exchanged solemn nods.

"Your friend wouldn't win any prizes with a rifle," Carmack commented. He drew his gun out and balanced it in his hand. "I'd spend a shell or two, if it was any my business."

"Wagon's got a water barrel on the tail."

"You've talked me into it."

The three riders, nervelessly practical as a seasoned execution squad, leveled their guns at the wagon and advanced their horses at a walk. "Hold it," Reagan told Carmack. He dismounted, sliding his .44 carbine from the saddle boot. He took aim. "Now!"

They fired together. The range was long for a handgun, though it ran downward, but by propping his wrist on his left forearm and lining the sights up steady to his eye Carmack dropped a bullet on the leg of a rider. Reflex action caused the rider to kick out wide and rearward, losing the stirrup and bringing his body bowing forward in the instinct for balance, so that his horse jumped confusedly broadside in the path of the man in the green silk shirt. Reagan's shot took the third man in the right shoulder. The punch of the blunt-nosed .44 jerked that one and made him pull trigger.

Instantly the man in the green shirt spun his horse and whirled off. He looked back up the slope, and over the sights of his carbine Reagan watched him rein from side to side furiously, zigzagging until he could put distance behind him.

The leg-shot man fell off his horse; or he appeared to, because his horse switched around under him as if to follow the leader, and out of the saddle he went. But he kept hold of the reins and managed to land on his good leg, with the horse closely covering him. A rifle twirled, swiftly unsheathed, and shrank to a searching muzzle, the barrel laid across the saddle. The man with the shoulder wound shook his head urgently. He plainly wanted to drop the matter without further damage.

11

Reagan set the hammer of the .44 carbine. There was fight in the leg-shot man. He couldn't do as the man in the green shirt had done so handily. His alternative was to fight, and he got off a shot that nicked the underedge of Reagan's trigger hand and cut the sleeve of his coat. Carmack said with irony, "Your friend in the wagon might've saved you that. He gun-shy?"

"Wasn't when I knew him," Reagan returned absently. After his flinch he realigned his sights and fired. His bullet screamed off the saddle. The man ducked, to reappear beneath the belly of his horse.

Reagan had his sights already waiting for him there. He fired once more. The horse swung around hindside, but was held from bolting by the reins caught under the arm of the man who now lay face down on the ground.

The remaining man stared up in speechless appeal, touching his wounded shoulder and again shaking his head. He was too hurt to try a dash, and had dropped his gun. The fact that he expected to be shot down in cold blood was a measure of his own merciless standards. Carmack raised a hand in a flicking gesture to him and glanced at Reagan, who shrugged. They watched him cross the hollow and climb his horse up the opposite ridge to where the man in the green shirt had halted out of gunshot range. The two riders held a brief conference, scanned the ominous sky westward, and moved on over the ridge.

In the silence a faint sound made itself audible. Carmack frowned, then his eyebrows arched above eyes wide with bewilderment. The sound continued, softly repetitive, feminine, definitely that of a woman's choking sobs.

"Now we'll look into the wagon," said Reagan.

Two

LEADING THE BLACK down the slope, Reagan carried the carbine cocked ready. Harby would be anything but pleased to see him. Besides, one never knew what turn of reaction a man might take at the end of a vicious dry-gulching. Or a woman, for the matter.

So he tipped the carbine up when the rear flap of the canvas top bulged. But the woman who jumped down off the tail gate didn't have a gun, and although she was sobbing she didn't give the impression of being completely off her head. Reagan heard Carmack expel breath in a wondering grunt. The woman seemed quite young. She had the glossy hair of a coppery color. Harby had good taste in women.

She came running toward them, making those choking sounds in her throat, eyes streaming, and Reagan veered off in swift impatience and let her go to Carmack. A squawling woman was an irritation at any time, twisting her fingers imploringly and making a big to-do. He thought that much of it was habit with the best of them, or unconscious affectation, and with the worst it was a self-interested bidding for any man's attention. Let Carmack take on that chore; it was time he did something toward earning his way.

Reagan didn't catch what she said first to Carmack, and he doubted if Carmack did, either. The words were broken by her sobbing, her breathlessness, and in frantic urgency she caught Carmack's arm and shook it as though he were being willfully stupid.

"Come quick—he's hurt! He's dying!"

Carmack ran with her to the wagon and climbed in, not pausing at the water barrel lashed on the tail gate.

Reagan drew a pail of water for the black and filled the dipper twice for himself. While he drank he ran his eyes over Harby's outfit, mechanically taking stock. Hay in a ground sheet slung beneath the high wagon bed, a sack of grain under the driver's seat, half a barrel of water, a grub box. Three good horses left of the team, and there was the mount of the man he'd had to shoot down. The black would soon pick up. Nothing wrong with it that some rest and care . . .

"I'm afraid he's gone." Carmack's voice reached him from inside the wagon. The woman, instead of crying out and raising hob about it, only made a small moaning sound.

Reagan hung up the tin dipper and went to secure the horse of the downed rider. He freed its reins and led it up to the wagon, and threw off its saddle. It was a roan, with white fetlock and stockings, bearing the brand of an H resting on a quarter circle. He stripped the harness off the three team horses and hung it on the wagon tongue. The saffron cloud was reaching almost overhead. He hoped to find gunny sacks in the wagon to help protect the heads of all five horses from the coming blast.

So Harby had got it. Had he caught up with the blue wagon thirty minutes sooner, Reagan mused, or twenty minutes, even ten... After four years, a few minutes had chopped off the sharp point of encounter. Thanks to turning aside for a sour stray. Well, Carmack couldn't be blamed for that. He hadn't begged for help. But damn him all the same, he had cost the loss between a near miss and a score that ran close to forty thousand dollars. Harby wasn't so careless as to carry the money on him, and only he would have known where he soaked it away. And now Harby was dead.

Reagan swung up onto the tail gate and raised the canvas flap. Ignoring Carmack and the woman, he looked down at the dead man between them. Harby had evidently tumbled backward off the driver's seat when he was hit, and fallen into the wagon, his head toward the rear. His shirt was blood-soaked. He had been shot in the chest, over the heart. Reagan pushed past Carmack for a look at the face.

It was the face of an unusually handsome man, the features all in balance proportion, lean but not thin except below the cheekbones, where the line of the jaw curved down to the cleft chin. Gray hair, but his years had not made him jowly or thick at the neck. Harby's face—yet with a difference, perhaps due to death and to the fact that his eyes were closed. It seemed much less hard, the chiseled lips less cynical.

"I don't see how he could shoot at all," Carmack muttered, "with a bullet through his heart."

Harby was not wearing a gun. Reagan looked at a rifle, the only visible weapon in the wagon, noting that it was a new Henry repeater with fancy trimmings. The sides of the breech were silvered and engraved, and an elaborate silver

14

plate was set into the stock. He lifted it and levered the action, ejecting an empty shell.

"He didn't shoot this," he remarked. Any shooter of experience would have levered in a fresh shell immediately after firing. Especially Harby, that rapid-fire marksman.

"No," the woman said. "I did." Both men looked at her. She was dry-eyed now, her face numb. She spoke without expression, in the manner of a half-awake child relating a dream. "They gave him the rifle the day we left home. He never fired it. Never fired a gun in his life. He only kept it because they presented it to him."

"Who?" Reagan asked.

"The people of our town."

Reagan's imagination boggled at the picture of townsmen presenting an expensive going-away gift to Harby, unless it was to get rid of him. "Why?"

The numbed face reflected a glimmer of resentment at the skeptical question. "They respected him. He was stern, yet—gentle."

Gentle, Reagan thought. Harby. *Gentle!* He dropped his eyes to the dead man's face, again observing its lack of sneering hardness. A feeling of uncertainty entered him. "Did he know those three were stalking him?" he asked the woman.

"No," she replied.

"Then why did he turn off east into these ridges?"

"He decided to search for the Phoenix stage road. At Ute a man told him this was the shorter route, but we seemed to be getting lost."

"He chose a poor place to change route," Carmack said.

Reagan nodded. Gullible and inept—Harby, of all men. Accepted a stranger's word, got lost, then worsened it. "For the Santa Cruz diggin's, I suppose?"

"No." Under his questioning she was emerging from her stunned apathy. "A town called Cochimi."

He studied her more closely, trying to make her out. She spoke well, in a soft voice. She wasn't as yet using the tricks of the trade, those beguiling tricks that could be expected of a kept woman who, losing her provider, promptly had to set about finding another. A young novice, perhaps, with much to learn.

"How long have you . . ." he began, but then the wagon became shaded as if a curtain had drawn over the sun. The backlash of the high wind boomed like distant cannon, while before it, in the maw under the racing dust cloud, the air

15

stilled as in the vortex of a cyclone. He leaped out of the wagon, calling to Carmack, "Tie down for the blow, quick!"

They huddled in the wagon, wet handkerchiefs over their mouths and nostrils, barely able to see each other through the thick dust. The canvas top, hastily roped down, bulged in tight as a drum on the windward side. Sand hissed and beat against it, and on the sheltered side the canvas billowed and snapped. The wagon swayed, creaking on chocked wheels, threatening to capsize under the pounding wind.

The storm would sweep on and be gone from here as suddenly as it struck, Reagan knew. How long it might last, though, nobody could foretell, and in its duration anything could happen. The hot, tearing blast raveled the nerves. Men got edgy, horses went wild, women became hysterical.

His last question, left unfinished, occurred to him. Thinking of it, he rephrased it and asked the woman, "How long did you know Harby?" She raised her head in a motion indicating that she didn't understand his words in all the noise, and he repeated them more loudly. He leaned toward her to catch her reply. His nose informed him that she was not wearing perfume, at least not of the overpowering kind familiar to dance halls.

"All my life, of course."

Baffled, he sat with his elbows on his knees and broodingly regarded her. "Where'd you and he come from?"

"A small town not far from Durango, up in Colorado."

"Live together there?"

"Of course."

Her "of course" rasped him unreasonably. The sandstorm, he thought; the damned sandstorm had him edgy. Her face, the lower half of it, was covered by her handkerchief. He studied her eyes searchingly at close range. Brown eyes. No, deep hazel. Clear, steady. They even looked guileless. "What was Harby doing there these last, say, four years?"

"What he's always done, of course. Teaching school. He was the schoolmaster there for the past eighteen years."

He sank back, his regard staying fixed on her. What was this? What the hell *was* this? In a moment he again leaned forward to her. "Why was he driving to Cochimi? Another job teaching school, maybe?"

His irony didn't get through to her. "No," she said. She began to sound strained. "He inherited a ranch near Cochimi. He thought it nicer for us to drive down, seeing the country, instead of taking the stage. He had never been out

16

of Colorado before, except East to school when he was young."

There were other schools Harby had gone to, Reagan mused. On the Texas-Mexico border and elsewhere. Not as a student. As a master of the hard-riding, fast-shooting school. And of the double-cross.

"Whose ranch did he inherit?"

Carmack had moved nearer and was listening to them. He shook his head at Reagan, and, touching the woman on her arm, he said something to her that Reagan missed. Because he had been the one to respond to her plea for help, and was first to enter the wagon, he apparently was assuming some sort of proprietary right to her and setting himself up as her new guardian. Reagan paid him a bleak stare.

The woman turned back to Carmack, and it was to him she spoke, defensively, as if sensing the atmosphere of skepticism and wanting someone to believe her. "It was his brother's ranch. I mean," she elaborated, "he inherited it through the death of his brother, who owned it. It's called the Rocking H. We rather expected somebody from it to meet us up at Ute."

"Somebody met you here instead," Reagan commented. "Those three. I didn't notice their horse brands, but the roan—the one they left behind—wears a Rocking H. Can you account for that?"

"Stolen," Carmack gave opinion. "Outlaws pick up horses anywhere they find 'em, as I guess you know. Quit bearing down on her." He patted her arm. "You don't have to tell us anything you don't want to."

Dust got into her nose and she sneezed. She wiped her nose. "I've got nothing to hide," she protested.

"Then you're one in a thousand," Reagan said. "What was the brother's name?"

"Amiel Harby."

Involuntarily taking a quick and incautious breath, Reagen also sneezed. After sitting silent for a moment, he muttered, "I be damned!" He nodded in the direction of the dead man. "Who's he?"

"Allen Harby."

"And you?"

"Susan Harby. My father and Uncle Amiel were twin brothers. Twins run in the family. I had a twin sister, but she died soon after birth."

"Allen Harby's your father?"

"Of course."

17

"I be damned!" he muttered again. Presently he rose and brought her a dipper of water. Carmack groped around until he found her a fresh handkerchief. The two small acts of kindness, following so suddenly after the hard attitude, caused a reaction. Susan Harby cried quietly. The two men, throughout the rest of the storm, stonily watched each other.

They wrapped Allen Harby in a blanket and buried him there. Susan Harby read the burial service. She spoke of his having always been an upright man, God-fearing, a gentle and understanding father. Toward the end her voice choked. When she had finished, Lew Reagan went to fight the roan into harness to take the place of the killed horse, leaving Carmack the job of filling in the grave.

Death and tears. He had come to look upon life as essentially a gamble, and gambling grew stale when not played to the limit. Always to win was not to be expected. To lose, finally, ended the game. As simple as that, no heartbreak entailed, no regrets. But Susan Harby was the dead man's daughter, of course, a young woman with a full measure of tender feelings and emotion. And it was doubtful that Allen Harby, schoolmaster, had ever knowingly gambled with his life.

Jim Carmack put up the spade and stepped around the wagon before Reagan was through teaching the roan the difference between saddle and harness. "What's on your mind, Reagan?"

"Stand, you goat!" Reagan clouted the fractious roan. "What? Why, it's in my mind to get this outfit rolling. Straighten out the trace chain."

Carmack unkinked the trace chain. "Rolling where?"

His tone drew him a sharp look from Reagan. "Out of these ridges and east to the stage road. What water's left in that barrel won't last long. We'll refill at a relay station."

"And then?"

"On down to Cochimi and that Rocking H ranch, where else?"

"I've been thinking," Carmack said slowly. "When I was filling in the grave, and halfway watching her, I thought to myself, 'Godamighty, she's all alone and helpless'!" He turned his head. "Look at her, kneeling there . . . She's young, only about eighteen. A girl. She's a long way from home, and she's too pretty for her own good. It was plain to me you figured her at first for a—"

18

"I grant she's young and pretty," Reagan interrupted him. "I don't grant she's alone. She's got help. She's better off now, strictly speaking, than she was with only her father. He seems to've been a green pilgrim, outside of school. Couldn't shoot, trusted strangers, and his driving was lousy. Pretty poor escort. I'm not. Don't know about you."

"I can get around."

"You were afoot when I found you, busted and cussing the world. It doesn't recommend you to me."

Carmack flashed. "Getting back to Susan—"

"Miss Harby?"

"All right—Miss Harby, then. If you made a mistake about her, others could do the same. Cochimi has gone tough, I hear, since the new diggings opened. I agree the stage road's our best bet from here. But there we ought to put her on a northbound stage and see she gets back safe to her home town up in Colorado."

Reagan smiled thinly. "You'd see she got there?"

"Well—"

"If she's Allen Harby's only living child, his death puts her first in line to claim the ranch. And maybe other valuable property. Such as cash. Amiel Harby never passed up a chance to fill his pockets, I happen to know."

"After she's home," Carmack argued, "she can get lawyers to—"

"That's going at it the long way round," Reagan said. "It might suit you, but not me—and frankly I judge I'm the one who's best qualified to look after her interests."

"Damn it, Reagan, you're taking a lot for granted!" Carmack exploded. "You forget she's got a say in the matter!"

Reagan shook his head. "No say at all," he said gently. "She needs help. What can she do by herself? She can't even handle the wagon alone. So we roll on down to Cochimi."

"It'll take all of three days getting there."

"Three days or a week, what difference to you? My 'we' didn't include anything so useless as a tramp on the make!"

His cutting blast, Reagan thought, had brought on a showdown, and he grimly welcomed it, for he tabbed Carmack as what he had called him. A tramp on the make. An interfering intruder with aims to improve at cheap cost his shabby lot. A potential nuisance, growing more insolent and pushy as he gained position. Give an inch, he would take a mile. Better to have it out with him, get rid of him at once.

Stiffening, the younger man thrust his head slightly forward and his hands became fists. His voice was a hoarse

19

whisper when at last he spoke. "Reagan, you made a mistake about her. You're making a mistake about me."

Reagan shook his head. "I guess not. Quit the pack any time, tramp, sooner the better!"

"Can you see me doing it? Another mistake. I'm sticking! Sticking close, all the way! My interest is personal."

"So's mine!"

"You've made that clear!"

Reagan waited, but Carmack turned away, heaving a sigh. Curling his lip, Reagan cuffed the roan, which was making efforts to climb over the wagon tongue, and went to saddle the black.

Three

JIM CARMACK estimated that it would take three days for them to reach Cochimi, but on the afternoon of the third day the wagon threw a wheel and compelled a delay for repairs. The stage road they found to be in bad condition, deeply rutted, cut by old washouts, and at the only relay station along their way they had to pay a surly tender for water and fill the barrel themselves. Grain was not for sale, but Reagan bought whiskey and stole a full morral while the tender went to get the bottle.

"It's hard country," he explained to Susan Harby, who seemed to think that he had done something dishonest. "That feller ought to keep his eyes open."

"But stealing is wrong!"

"Not this kind of stealing. A man's got to look out for his horses. If he doesn't he's a tramp." His glance touched Jim Carmack.

Sundown caught them some ten miles short of Cochimi. To push on after dark would have been senseless, on that road, so they pulled off and made camp for the night. Carmack had taken on the driving of the wagon from the start, and to him fell the work of stripping and attending the team. Susan Harby set about preparing the evening meal.

Reagan, riding the black, had gathered up scraps of wood along the route and tossed them into the back of his wagon. He scooped a shallow hole in the ground, placed a few stones around the edge, and carried the wood and the Dutch oven to it. Women in general, he believed, had no knack for building a really successful fire outdoors. A woman's fire was a smoky affair, fated to sulk and burn unevenly, becoming hot as a furnace after the cooking was ruined. The fire he built was economical, Indian style, flat on top and level with the stones. The flames spread through the bottom kindling, enveloped the top layer of larger pieces, and in minutes it was a cook fire with a minimum of smoke. Squatting on his heels by it, he uncorked the whiskey bottle and took his first drink in several days, a deep one, swallowing slowly on the fierce bite of it.

Susan Harby came from the wagon, bearing pans and coffeepot, and he regarded her thoughtfully. So young, yet so much a woman, lithe-limbed, an unconscious pride of womanliness causing her to walk almost too erectly. Behind her the after-rays of the dipped sun framed her in a soft glow, and Reagan, his eyes trapped by curve and contour, rose to his feet as she came near.

She paused. Holding the pans and coffeepot before her, she looked at him uncertainly. That she was a little afraid of him he knew; perhaps more than a little. She had not forgotten his initial hardness of attitude toward her. The first faint breeze of evening was rising. A wisp of smoke blew into her face. He realized then that he was occupying the windward side of the fire and he moved back to give her the position. She sank down, arranged her skirts, and went to work on the meal. He stood gazing down at the back of her head.

Across his mind there moved the shadow of a discontent that he thought he had left far behind. It had haunted him badly at one time, until he learned to avoid introspection. And here it came at him again, stirring up memories of neglected ambitions, of the forgotten things he once had wanted and had abandoned. This girl had raised the ghost, damn it, simply by sitting at a fire that he had built. Cooking their evening meal. At his fire. Like a bride...

He cleared his throat and said gruffly to her, "I take it you don't have a mother."

The man would be fortunate who won this girl. In surrender she would be glorious, giving him all her trust, all her faith and loyalty. She was full-hearted. Though not yet gay, she had accepted the fact of her father's death and healthily overcome the shock of it. No more tears. She had strength of character, a resiliency of spirit that was infinitely better than brittle hardness.

Too occupied to look around at him, or too conscious of him, standing behind her, she shook her head without raising it. "No. My mother died when I was six, and my father never married again."

"Any relatives?"

"Distant relatives." She laughed a little wryly. "Very distant. They're the kind of people who think education is only good for making money, and my father was an educated man who didn't earn very much as a teacher. They considered him a failure."

"Did he ever try ranching?"

"No. He wasn't very practical, I'm afraid, except in his profession."

22

Did things the hard way. Not like his brother Amiel, who always found the easy way. "His brother was different," Reagan observed.

She looked around and up at him then. "You sound as if you knew him." When Reagan didn't respond, she said, "Yes, altogether different, according to my father. I never met him. He traveled about the country on business, and wrote to my father a few times, but he never visited us."

She turned back to the fire, busying herself. Watching the play of her hands, Reagan detected unsureness, a trembling haste that betrayed her into making wasted motions. He balanced on the edge of a powerful temptation to reach down and take her into his arms, to test her reaction. She was, as Carmack had said, alone, and her beauty could easily bring her to grief. And there was her inheritance. No close relatives. The young and inexperienced daughter of a small-town schoolmaster. She needed guarding. Needed a man, a seasoned man capable of holding his own, able to ...

A sound behind the wagon drew his thoughts up short. He drank again from the bottle, silently damning Carmack's hindering presence in camp. Another question occurred to him.

"Who was it your father expected to meet up at Ute?"

"The lawyer from Cochimi. He offered to, late last year when we first learned of my uncle's death, but we couldn't leave then because there was nobody to take over the school. When we were ready my father wrote and told him when we expected to reach Ute. I suppose he was too busy to meet us."

Reagan shrugged. Most likely the lawyer had assumed that Allan Harby was as tough as his brother Amiel, perfectly able to make a journey without getting himself into a damn'-fool bobble. That lawyer would have a further job because of it, establishing Susan's legal claim to the property. Reagan wondered what kind of ranch the Rocking H might be and what Amiel Harby had done with the money he had taken out of Texas four years ago.

The last daylight faded, and the evening breeze steadied and hugged close to the ground. Reagan stepped around to the other side of the fire. In the swiftly deepening dusk he watched the firelight on Susan's face. She couldn't help knowing that his eyes were on her, and he intended for her to know it and to know his thoughts. His campaign would be fast, forceful as soon as she wavered, binding her to him. Cochimi tomorrow. He distrusted lawyers. The lawyer would

23

press advice upon her, take up her interests, raise obstacles to prevent her and the property from being won by a stranger.

He silently pitted his will to force her to look up at him, but she kept her head bent to her tasks, though her face flushed hotly and her hands performed superfluous acts. Suddenly her hands faltered and went still. Her lips began quivering. Tears sprang to her eyes. She looked across the fire at his booted feet, and slowly lifted her gaze. He was winning, he told himself. Winning . . .

Jim Carmack strode to the fire, carrying a lighted lantern that threw his leg-shadows in scissoring patterns over the gound. He set the lantern down and sat on his heels beside Susan. He lifted the coffeepot. Susan expelled breath like the gasp of a swimmer surfacing from deep water, and exclaimed, "It's hot!"

Putting the coffeepot down, he blew on his fingers. "So it is." He used his handkerchief in grasping the handle again, and looked up at Reagan. "Coffee with your whiskey?"

Reagan only stared down at him. Dourly. Ominously. Something had to be done about this pushy tramp.

Presently Susan and Carmack were talking quietly together, making a joint project of getting the meal ready. Leaning against a wagon wheel, occasionally drinking from the bottle, Reagan held his patience. Carmack behaved very much at ease with Susan. And she with him.

At lot more than she is with me, Regan reflected, and he was not displeased by it. A man didn't want such a girl to be entirely at ease in his company. Not if he was out to win her. That gasp of hers had been a gasp of relief at the interruption, certainly. She was shy and afraid of surrender, and Carmack's intrusion had broken the spell, given her an opening to retreat onto safe ground.

Next time, no interruption. Something had to be done. Tonight.

Jim Carmack had aligned himself with Susan Harby right from the start, against Lew Reagan's unfeeling attitude toward her, and now that the older man was on a different tack Carmack was more than even Susan's self-elected protector. Long after the evening meal they stayed talking together, Carmack feeding the fire, until a dismal howl in the distance snatched Susan's gaze away from the flames.

Night had cooled the air. Prussian blue, the sky was like velvet, jeweled with a full moon and blue-white stars, and in their pale light the stage road to Cochimi lay as a winding band cast down onto a dead land. Tall sahuaros were gaunt sentinels left by some doomed and forgotten era, spreading their arms upward forever in motionless entreaty. The faraway howl splintered into a yapping chorus.

"Coyotes," Jim Carmack said. "They'll circle us. Our fire gets them curious. Might be a dog or two in the pack, gone wild. They won't come near."

Susan had heard coyotes many times, but she shivered. Their frenetic cry was one of the night sounds back home on the outskirts of town, as familiar as the crowing of roosters at full moon. These did not sound the same. Their cry, here in the dead land, carried a foreboding quality, sinisterly gleeful, demoniac. She bade Carmack good night and retired into the wagon. Carmack sat on by the fire.

Lew Reagan rose from lying fully dressed on a saddle blanket, on the far side of the tethered horses, and walked into the firelight. "Time we had a talk," he said tonelessly. He took note that Carmack got immediately to his feet as if waiting for this.

"If you say so." Carmack's face was taut with the knowledge of impending trouble.

"Cochimi tomorrow," Reagan said. "We split up tonight. I've had enough of your company."

"You're pulling out?"

Chill humor glinted in Reagan's eyes. "No. You are!"

Carmack looked away. He said factually, "I'm a Wyoming cowman. Or was. A barbed-wire fence put some of us to fighting, and after burying my father I got the man who killed him. But we lost, so I left Wyoming. The barbed-wire crowd wasn't satisfied. They sent a pair of gunmen after me. The pair caught up with me in Salt Lake City and we shot it out. The Mormons didn't approve. I had to grab the first horse handy and get out of Utah."

"You're trying to tell me you're big with a gun?"

"No. You're the one who's big in that line, if I suspect right. I've met your kind a time or two. What I'm trying to tell you is, I'm through running. Had enough of it. You can't run me off, Reagan!"

"You want to die?"

"I'll risk it." Carmack brought his eyes back to Reagan. "You mean that, don't you? I'm in your way—standing in your way to what you want—and you'd kill me to get your damn' paws on—"

"Let it go!" Reagan snapped. "We've had our talk." He jerked the strip of handkerchief off his bullet-nicked hand.

25

The partly healed wound was dry, and when he worked his fingers it cracked open and blood came. The small mishap honed the edge of his anger. "Back up and draw, you fool, or quit camp!"

Jim Carmack, taking a slow step backward, dropped his eyes to Reagan's middle. He had observed that under his coat Reagan wore two guns, butts forward, in cutaway holsters hung from a single belt. A gun fighter. A cross-draw man. He said with intense seriousness, "I've got to stop you, Reagan. I'll get a bullet into you somehow—"

"Back up and draw, then!"

They back-stepped, facing each other. By unspoken agreement they halted while the campfire between them still held them in its light, ten steps apart. Reagan surveyed Carmack's stance, his eyes, the position of his right hand. A fighting cowboy. Dangerous as such, but his trade was not built on his gun. Didn't really want this showdown. Would go through with it, though, believing that he had a chance. For a woman.

His anger suddenly cooling to sarcasm, Reagan said, "You've gone noble since I raked you off the lid of hell! It was dog eat dog, then. And now?"

Carmack shook his head ever so slightly, his eyes pinned on Reagan's right hand. "Not noble. Just ordinary human, grateful to be alive so I can—"

"Grateful? What's that?" Reagan threw back at him his own words. "Nobody does anything for anybody without there's a profit, remember?" He nodded toward the wagon. "There's the profit, you hungry dog! Her! Your noble sentiments don't impress me like your nerve does, trying to jump my claim! I give you a last chance to be on your way. You can take the roan."

"You've got no claim on her!"

Words of reason were wasted on a fool, and to offer him a chance to back out was, Reagan guessed, taken as a sign of weakness, of bluffing. "Damn!" he muttered. Aloud he said with a trace of weariness. "All right, cowboy, get to it . . ."

As he spoke, he heard the harsh rustle of canvas, and on the edge of his vision he saw Susan drop from the wagon. Polished metal mirrored a flash of firelight. He cut his eyes to her. She came forward, holding the silver-mounted Henry repeater in both hands, level with her waist.

"Stop it!" she said. "Stop it!" The two men turned their faces toward her, and she halted as though meeting a physical impact. She was very white, holding the rifle pointed between

26

them, her gaze flitting from one to the other. In a falling voice she said again, "Stop it!"

Nobody spoke for a full minute. The rifle was hammer-cocked. Her finger was on the trigger. The combination of distraught woman and loaded firearm was not a comforting one for Reagan to contemplate, and he shifted his balance. At once the muzzle pointed at him. He considered the slight trigger pressure of a cocked Henry, the hole that the .44-caliber ball could make in his stomach, and wished that Susan were a man. In something of a quandary, he spared a glance at Carmack to see if he was about to take advantage of the situation.

Carmack's hands hung at his sides. Reagan revised his opinion of him as a complete fool who was blunderingly out of his element when not neck-deep in cows. Carmack wasn't making any move that would bring that rifle to bear on him. His whole attention clung closely to Susan.

"Nobody has any claim on me! Nobody!" She spoke directly to Reagan. Her eyes flashed. Her small chin pushed out and the curve of her lips straightened. The cocked Henry stayed steady. "Why do you say you have? How dare you!" It was obvious that she thought he was basing a presumptuous claim because of the hold he had exerted over her earlier in the evening. She was denying her momentary weakness before him.

"Because," he said, "in a way I do have a claim on you."

"You don't."

Carmack took the opportunity to move his right arm. He did it quietly, not especially fast, making a normal gesture of lifting his gun out of its holster. "You sure don't!" he stated, and Suan only glanced at his drawn gun and back at Reagan.

Reagan quelled his surge of wrath, forcing himself to weigh the matter detachedly. Bad deal, thanks to his reluctance to shoot Carmack and be done with it. Carmack and Susan were now joined against him, and no gunplay possible . . . Carmack, yes. Susan, no. Talk, then. Talk, dammit, and watch for a break. Get the cowboy off guard, drop him, and jump for the rifle.

He said casually and truthfully to Susan, "I knew Amiel Harby four years ago in Texas. We operated along the border, recovering wet cattle. Rustlers were stealing Texas cattle and selling them in Mexico by the herd. We'd go down and get the cattle back, for a price."

27

"Sounds easy," Carmack commented, interested. "How about the Mexican buyers, though?"

"They objected. With," Reagan added, "gun smoke, more and more often. They were getting smart to us, and we knew the game couldn't last. We were pooling most of our money, to keep any of us from flashing a roll—those Texas cowmen weren't ever grateful at having to pay us the reward for the return of their cows, and if they saw us too prosperous it led to trouble. We agreed to quit and split it up among us when it reached fifty thousand dollars."

"I don't believe it!" Susan declared flatly. "Uncle Amiel, my father's own twin brother, mixed up in such things?"

Reagan shrugged. "It was a legitimate business, only rough." Feigning abstractedness, he let his gaze drift to Carmack's gun. A single-action Colt, altered from cap-and-ball to center-fire. Cowboy gun, heavy, not designed for speed. Jim Carmack held it hanging in his hand, muzzle down. That was break enough, if it weren't for that damned rifle.

"Our last trip down, Harby said he was sick and he stayed behind," Reagan went on, brushing a look over the rifle. It was starting to droop, heavy in Susan's hands. "Coming back out of Mexico with a herd, we met trouble. A posse jumped us."

"You said it was a legitimate business!" Susan reminded him tartly.

"I did," he concurred. "And it was. But somebody had gone and sworn we were working both ends of the game—that we were doing the rustling ourselves and then bringing the stolen cattle back for the reward. He was one of us. Those Texas cowmen believed him. They were the posse, too mad to spit, thinking they'd been rooked by a gang of outsiders. The joke was on us. When we got home after the fight we found our cache cleaned out! Forty thousand dollars gone! Then we had to light out on the long dodge, Rangers on our tails."

"Uncle Amiel too?"

"He was already gone. Skipped out with our money, after he set the law on us and told the posse where to jump us!"

"It's a lie!"

"Great joker, your uncle," Reagan said reminiscently. "Pity he's dead. I promised myself, if I ever cut his trail, we'd have quite a party. Only a few days ago somebody told me he'd been seen driving through Ute, southbound in a blue wagon. With a woman—a fancy woman wearing a red dress."

28

"What?" Susan's face flamed. "My red dress—"

"Mistake. It was your father and you. Natural mistake, though, your father being Amiel Harby's twin brother. And a red dress in a blue wagon ... Anyhow, that's how I came to be trailing along, not by chance. Carmack, here, is just a stray burr that stuck to the blanket."

"Thanks," said Camrack dryly. "This stray burr is sticking till—"

"Even if you're telling the truth," Susan broke in, "what claim do you have on me?"

He had not furthered his purpose, Reagan realized, by his reference to the red dress and to her having been mistaken for a loose Lulu. The whiskey in him had quickened his impulse to shock her; she looked so insufferably virtuous, telling him that he lied about her precious Uncle Amiel. Aroused, she raised the muzzle of the rifle in an unconscious reaction of protest at the slander. Nevertheless, along with her challenging question, her face registered a stir of wholly feminine curiosity.

The pointing rifle exasperated him. He answered her in a deliberate drawl. "Your uncle is dead and I can't collect from him. Your father inherited your uncle's property. He's dead too. You inherit from your father—and you're very much alive, Susan Harby!"

"Your claim isn't on me at all! It's the property, only the property—"

"On you, yes! You'll be owning Amiel Harby's property, part of which I lay claim to! I take the right to protect my personal interests!"

"Your interests! You mean because I'm only a woman you think you can—can—"

"Rob you? Make you my woman? I wouldn't bother to cook up lies about it first! Nor would the next man. Putting it plain, you're too young and way too attractive to let run around unguarded in this forsaken country. You need a guardian. Lay down that rifle!"

The rifle sagged, she staring down at it, her color high, and Reagan took a step toward her.

Carmack's drawn gun sliced up. "No, you don't!" Reagan jerked his head, and Carmack, meeting his glare, said to Susan, "Stand clear of him! Don't you see what he's trying at? Look at him! He's a killer!"

She raised one startled look at Reagan's darkly scowling face. "Killer?" she said, and then, "Jim!" She went to stand

29

partly behind Jim Carmack, and from there peered as if shortsighted at the tall man standing beyond the campfire.

Reagan looked at them both, at the gun and rifle turned on him, and at their eyes. This, said memory, had happened to him before, in another place and at another time. Two in league against the devil. It had happened as the finality to the accrued evidence of small things: hushed voices, furtive meetings of glances, smiles without meaning . . .

Self-disgust came to him abruptly. His talk of protecting his interests, of seeking only to recover what was his from Harby's property, was a lying cloak to his actual intentions. He had been trying to turn back the clock, trying for one more chance to regain what was lost and gone.

It was the cheap and shoddy aspect of it, not the morals, that revolted him. He, Lew Reagan, had tried to better himself at a woman's expense, like a tramp on the make, and God only knew how far he might have gone with it if Carmack had not stood pat.

He walked out of the firelight toward the horses, and the gun and rifle pointed after him until he said over his shoulder, "Luck," to the pair standing together watching him. Carmack, correctly taking the single word as a definite farewell, and aware that the departure was voluntary rather than forced by firearms, lowered his gun and responded, "Luck."

Reagan went directly to the black and fitted on saddle and bridle. He drained the bottle and threw it away, and, hearing it crash among stones, he felt that he had drunk a toast at a funeral. He mounted and rode out of camp, not letting himself look back at Susan and Carmack, not too sure that it wouldn't change his mind even now if Susan should just happen to wave a hand in that man-disturbing way that came naturally to some women. Perhaps it wasn't always intentional, but when they fluttered their fingers in the air for farewell, a man could read it as a subtle signal that he'd be welcome back.

Pushing his thoughts forward, he smiled dimly over the brief meditation that it was he, not Carmack, who was heading on south to the Santa Cruz diggings. Still, it was a good thing, Carmack standing pat. Showed he had nerve and could stick. He might even make Susan a good husband.

As for the money, let it go. Maybe Harby had spent the forty thousand, anyway, before his death. "Or put it in cows!" Reagan murmured. He grunted at the thought of Harby as a respectable cattleman, wishing that he could have walked in on Harby and settled the score. Well, that was past wishing for, and this trek could still be made profitable. Gold flowed fast in the mining camps. Sooner he got there and into the swim the better. Needed a fresh stake.

He fingered the money belt under his shirt. Pretty lean, but enough left for seed. The harvesting would depend on his wits.

Suddenly he hungered for a cigar, and he touched the black to a canter before it occured to him that this was a case of hurry up and wait. Cochimi had to sleep sometime, and that would be about the time he rode in, a couple of hours before sunup, everything in town closed. Vainly searching his pockets, he scowled.

"Damn! Not even a smoke..."

Four

SOUTH OF TOWN the road bent away from a line of hills and ran on through low-growing patches of dusty chaparral that stretched like a worn-out blanket, dark green, the holes strewn with rocks as starkly gray as steel in the morning sun. Unfruitful country, hopelessly barren, yet the air carried a hint of moisture. The prevailing air currents came from off the hills, and Reagan guessed that on the far side the country was different, blessed by springs or a stream. It lay off his course and he didn't need water this morning. Presently a fork in the road ahead confirmed his idle guess. The fork cut toward a cleft in the hills. Some habitable land over there, possibly cattle country, unlike these worthless wastes. He didn't have a high regard for this part of Arizona.

Cochimi had frayed his patience. As late as five in the morning everybody in town was asleep or dead drunk, or both. To get his horse fed and rubbed down, he finally had to pound on the livery doors until he woke up the stableman, who bellowed complaints. The noise brought several individuals stumbling out of a large establishment called the Hi Jolly, although the place was dark and apparently closed. They shouted at him, and he started to make their acquaintance, thinking that he glimpsed a green shirt among them, but at that moment the local deputy sheriff came along and an argument ensued.

Breakfast had entailed further waiting and some slight friction with a café cook who thought the hour too early for business. After another wait for the general store to open, Reagan bought his supplies and a spare canteen at prices evidently raised especially for him by the tight-faced storekeeper. By the time he got ready to leave he was soured on Cochimi. A lively town from all reports, one he ordinarily would have favored; but unfriendly. That deputy sheriff ...

A box buggy with red wheels, drawn by a pair of matched duns, swung into sight along the fork and came bowling toward the main road at a spanking rate of speed. The top of the buggy was up, shading the man who was driving and the woman beside him. It was shiny black, like the buggy itself and the polished harness. A two-horse team to a light rig was rare enough to catch the eye, and Reagan reined in to watch, curious to see what kind of man would own such a flashy turnout in this benighted land. The duns were pacers, beautifully gaited and full of go, but as he watched their action they broke gait and he saw the driver tightening up on the lines as if minded to halt. The raised top prevented Reagan from seeing the man clearly. The man could see him, though, sitting his horse on the main road.

"Looking me over," Reagan muttered. "Well, if I'm making you nervous I'll mosey along."

A perverse mood restrained him. There was a possibility that he was known to the man. Or to the woman. The buggy had not halted. It was coming on, though slowly, the team at a walk. His eyes were on the woman, who, seated on the sunny side and becoming visible to him, gave him the impression that she was Spanish. Her eyes were dark, her hair black, and there was a certain richness of dress. The man leaned forward and let the sun strike his face.

Reagan blinked once, his eyes widening. Then he blanked out all expression and touched his hat to the woman as the buggy drew up before him. To the man he said, " 'Lo, Frank."

Smiling gravely, Frank Tillander said, "Long time, Lew." And he gazed off into the distance like a man reviewing in his mind's eye the sentimental aspects of the past. "Four years, isn't it?"

"Since we split up, broke. You seem to've prospered."

"Can't complain. You?"

"So-so."

Frank Tillander had a pale skin that together with his light blue eyes and very fair hair, lent him the appearance of mildness. He wore a gray suit, its excellent tailoring wasted on his gangling frame. It did not save him from looking cumbersome and awkward. The look was deceptive. Reagan knew that Tillander could move as fast and surely as the next man.

The woman ran her dark eyes alertly from one to the other, having noticed that they had not shaken hands, and knowing they were sparring. Frank Tillander said, "Lew, this is Mrs. Plevin. Felisa—Mr. Reagan."

She arched her eyebrows. "Longrider Reagan? You've mentioned him to me, Frank."

"That Longrider thing," Reagan said, "was hung on me after an unfortunate bobble in Texas. I don't use it. Neither do my friends."

33

"Sorry." The tip of her tongue darted nervously over her lips.

Tillander kept his grave smile. "No harm done, Felisa. Mr. Reagan and I never pretended to be close friends. Just —business associates. Reminds me, Lew. Ever hear anything of the old bunch?"

"Not any more," Reagan told him. "After Texas they got careless. Mike Estaver and the Pomo tried train-robbing. The Lane boys were hanged with Black Jack in the mill at Ida. Hagan got in some kind of trouble in Mexico. I ran into Old Tim Farnley a while ago up in Ute, but he was burned out, swamping in a deadfall for his drinks."

"Pity. It was a great bunch."

The duns stamped restlessly and shook their heads, and Reagan's black, an older horse, flicked its ears at them. Tillander was holding the lines in his left hand, and now he used both to steady the team, first sliding a glance at Reagan's hands. "A great bunch," he repeated.

So, Reagan thought; meeting me has given him a shock. He hardly knows what to make of it and is waiting for me to speak of Harby. He's fishing to find out if I know about Harby coming way down here. And the woman, Felisa— Mrs. Plevin—is uneasy. She knows something of the score. Is there any Mr. Plevin around? No bets on that.

"Been to the diggin's yet?" Reagan asked.

"Santa Cruz?" Tillander nodded. "That where you're going?"

"Thought I'd take a whirl."

"You won't stay long. You'll soon be coming back." The words were spoken thoughtfully. All the best claims are worked by a mining syndicate."

"I didn't figure to dig in the muck."

"No, but it's the same with the gambling. The syndicate controls the settlements, tight. They pick their own men. Those who like outside talent come to Cochimi."

"When did you come here, Frank?" Reagan put the question casually, but he saw the woman freeze up as still as an image.

"Last year."

"About the time Harby died, was it?"

The woman sucked in a sharp breath, and Tillander bent over the lines, wrapping them twice over his left hand; then the light blue eyes rose, masked in a mockery of innocence. "Shortly before."

"How did he die?"

34

"Don't you know? Anybody around here could tell you. Didn't you ask in Cochimi?"

"You tell me."

The woman shifted ever so slightly, pressing her arm against the man beside her in the buggy. She kept her dark eyes fixed on Reagan's face. Tillander turned his head a little and said, "It's no secret. Everybody knows Harby stepped out his front door one fine morning and met a bullet."

"Somebody beat me to it," Reagan commented. "Who?"

Tillander shrugged. "As we used to say on the border— *Quién sabe?* Used a rifle. Nobody saw him. Just one shot"— he spread his right hand, closed it, and snapped thumb and finger—"and away. Gone. Could've been anybody, eh?"

"Could," Reagan said. He ranged a deliberate inspection over the fine dun horses, the flashy rig, the expensively dressed woman. "Did you get to pick up the forty thousand dollars he rascalled us out of?"

Tillander stretched his smile wide. "Not a cash dollar of it, believe me, Longrider—Lew, I mean—if I had it I'd split it with you." In the next breath, he asked, "How'd your hand get nicked? You been in a fight lately?"

Letting the question fall unanswered, Reagan lifted his reins and said, "Reckon I'll give the diggin's a look, anyway, seeing I've come this far. How do I get there?"

"Several ways. Best is to follow the road to Blanco, then southeast over the Piedras Gordas. I've got business today in Cochimi, or I'd invite myself along. One thing about us, we could generally figure things out together and find the hole in the other man's game. Look me up when you come back."

"Sure. We'll figure out the hole where the forty thousand went."

"We'll try, Longrider. Lew, I mean. Excuse me," Tillander apologized politely. He gave slack to the lines and the box buggy shot forward. The top had a small rear window, and through the isinglass Reagan glimpsed the woman's face, turned to stare back at him.

He touched his hat solemnly, grinning after the face quickly withdrew. His last remark to Tillander had been nothing but sarcasm, and its effect grimly amused him. It had worried the woman; she was sharing Tillander's prosperity, knew its source, and feared losing it. They were living high on that forty thousand, or on whatever part of it Tillander had managed to grab.

With a rifle, from ambush. Harby had deserved no better

35

end, but still it was a treacherous way to pay off a score. Reagan shook his head, the sick disgust creeping up in him again. The old bunch had gone bad, damned bad, and Frank Tillander wasn't any exception, his elegant trappings regardless. It wasn't all Harby's fault. Harby had cheated and betrayed them, put the outlaw mark on them, but afterward it was they who kicked the fence down. A man went lobo if he didn't draw the line somewhere. And he, himself...

He touched the black forward, past the fork and on down the road. Whether or not he made the grade in the Santa Cruz, he wasn't ever coming back this way. Not ever.

The blue wagon, three of its team pulling hard in the ruts, the sulking roan laying off, lumbered slowly into the main street of Cochimi. "Here at last!" Jim Carmack said, driving, and beside him Susan Harby echoed dubiously, "At last." They looked about them.

Jim Carmack saw it at first as simply another cowtown, much the same as others he had known. The same drabness, more so here than in Wyoming, because down here everything was built of unplaned lumber and the desert sun bleached all boards to a fuzzy gray. The same ramshackle look of a place begun as a makeshift and grown to permanence by slipshod additions. Presently he noticed some differences between it and a hundred others, and didn't like what he saw. Too many idling men for this busy time of year, and at midday the saloons were already noisy. This was a cowtown that had got itself swamped by the backwash of the Santa Cruz gold boom. He could only imagine what Susan, coming from a solid and respectable farming town, was thinking of it.

The steep main street bent and gave way to the thrusting front of Cochimi's largest building, a new saloon-and-hotel that bannered the name of Hi Jolly. The name, a corruption of Haj Alli, cropped up frequently in this part of the territory, for Haj Alli had been the Arab who came in with the camels for the Camel Corps, that ill-fated inspiration of Jefferson Davis.

It was a blatant offense, the manner in which the Hi Jolly took up all the boardwalk and part of the street, and the fact that it was tolerated in that spot indicated the importance of saloonkeepers in this town. Driving slowly past it on the uphill grade, Jim Carmack hailed a bearded man who stood half facing the low swing doors of the barroom, talking over them to somebody inside.

"Looking for a lawyer named Oakes—Mr. Jeffrey K. Oakes. Where's his office?"

The bearded man turned. His beard was cut square and he had cold eyes, and pinned to his vest was the badge of a deputy sheriff. He leveled a look at Jim Carmack, moved it on to Susan, wonderingly, and ran it over the wagon and team before he spoke.

"Old Jeff's office? Under his hat, when he wore it." His roving scrutiny stilled, fastened on the brand of the roan horse. "Now there's a queer thing. What's your name, young feller, and where'd you pick up that jughead?"

Two men walked quietly past the wagon, coming from behind. They caught the heads of the leaders, halting the team, while a third man chocked the rear wheels to prevent the wagon from rolling backward downhill. Other men drifted forward to look on.

"Don't tell him, Sam!" Susan whispered, suddenly fearful, and Jim said to the deputy, "I asked you where we can find Oakes."

"And I asked you your name!"

A man pushed through the swing-doors, saying as he emerged, "Let's not get officious, Heckels!" He was big and soft-spoken, a gangling man in a gray suit. He lifted his hat to Susan, paid her a long look that was more than a compliment, and said to Jim, "Mr. Oakes is no longer with us, I'm sorry to say."

"You mean he's dead?"

"He drank methylated spirits by mistake last Christmas and passed on to his reward. Can I help you? My name is Tillander."

More men were gathering to scan the wagon outfit, the driver and girl, and the roan. A few of them had the cut of working cowmen, and these, holding themselves aloof from the common run, seemed disposed on general principle to lend moral support to Heckels, for the deputy sheriff won their nods by declaring, "I'm the law officer here and I'm asking him a question, Mr. Tillander—*if* you don't mind!"

But the deputy's assertiveness was weakened by a petulant note in his voice, and something very much like amused contempt rippled across Tillander's pale face. Casting up the situation, Jim concluded that Tillander was a big man here, the right man to have on his side. To draw the man further over, he said to him, "My name's Carmack. This is Miss Harby." Realizing that he had posed an obvious question, he

37

added hastily, "I'm just her driver, is all. How do we get to the Rocking H ranch?"

"That's different," Heckels said obscurely. He regarded Susan with frowning interest. The cowmen in the crowd exchanged questioning looks.

The deputy made to speak again, but Tillander, smiling, cut him off. "It is, isn't it? Welcome—ah—Miss Harby!" He paid her another long look, one that brought a flush to her face. "Take the main road out to Papago Hills," he told Jim, "and turn east at the fork there. You can't miss it. Let go the team, you men. Some of you shove at the wheels and give Mr. Carmack a start. Any official objections, Heckels?"

Reluctantly, heavily, the deputy shook his head. "No objections, Mr. Tillander." He looked defeatedly at the men heaving at the wagon wheels, and trudged off, not replying to some of the cowmen who spoke to him.

Driving up the steep street, Jim stuck his head out and looked back. The crowd was dispersing, wandering back into the saloon, and Mr. Tillander was gone. "A middling-good town gone bad," he commented. "Never yet heard of cow country getting any benefit from a gold strike. It brings in the worst."

"Mr. Tillander..." Susan moved her shoulders as if to ease a weight on them. "I didn't like him!"

"He did me a good turn. The deputy had jail in his eye, 'count of this Rocking H roan, I could see that. Tillander steered him off my neck."

"Yes, but for a minute I couldn't help wishing Lew Reagan hadn't left us."

"A good thing he did," Jim countered sharply. "Lawmen can spot a bad man. It's something they learn, like a gambler learns to read a man's face and know if he's holding top cards. I've an idea Reagan's posted on a few dodger bills. He'd have done us more harm than good, maybe by blasting down the deputy! Forget about Reagan."

"I suppose," Susan said, "that's what the deputy spotted about you."

"You're wrong there. I'm no bad man!"

"What are you?"

"A cowman who ran into tough luck and had to jump."

"Isn't that what Lew Reagan is?"

"No!" Jim snapped. "He's a gambler and gun fighter, and God knows what else, if I'm any judge!"

38

"You're not a judge," said Susan, deliberately and perversely misinterpreting him; "luckily for the rest of us!"

They rode on in seething silence after that. The town dropped far behind and the country opened out, a barren vastness that called for remark, but neither of them had a word to say to the other. A string of distant riders bobbed in and out of hidden folds in the terrain, evidently a ranch crew headed home, southward from Cochimi. They passed from view, soon followed by a couple of stragglers riding hard to catch up with them. Watching them, Jim Carmack felt a tug of regret for the lost Wyoming days, for the deep satisfactions of working in familiar places with lifelong friends. The wild ride home after the monthly trip to town, pockets empty; the pranks and rollicking horseplay...

He hit the stubborn roan with the whip, and Susan, thinking it an expression of ill temper, set her face straight ahead and remained resolutely mute.

The afternoon was half spent when they turned off at the fork, and by the time the wagon crawled through Papago Hills the sun hung well down behind them. Then they were entering a great sweep of range that fell away in long folds, threaded by streams, a land as different from the land they had just left as day from night. Papago Hills formed a natural barrier between high chaparral and low range. Here was grass, growing green in the moist pockets, as gold elsewhere as ripe wheat, and there were actual trees, cottonwoods and willows, clumps of them.

It was a rare sight. Jim Carmack drank it in, keenly aware of how he had been thirsting for something like this. This was real cow country, stretching out for miles, unfenced. He knew that it must be all taken up by ranches, and he envied the owners. Cattle were plodding out of the shady hollows as the sun sank down. Roundup would present no problem on such open range, if the ranchers worked together. The wagon trundled past the last shoulder of hill and he saw the buildings of a ranch, a trail leading to them. He swung the team onto the trail, and spoke to Susan.

"Who's been running things since your uncle died, d'you know?"

She shook her head. "Mr. Oakes wasn't very clear in his letters, and his writing was terrible. He sent my uncle's will and some other papers..."

"They here in the wagon?"

"No. My father left them with a lawyer back home. But he brought copies and identification papers, of course."

By their size the ranch buildings they approached bespoke a fairly large outfit. The house itself was modest, but there was a long bunkhouse, new, a combination barn and blacksmith shed, and extensive corrals and pens beyond the bare yard. The high crossbeam above the gate had the brand of the Rocking H burned into it. Jim drove under it into the yard and hauled the team to halt. One of the pens held some horses whose coats were still streaked from recent riding. He guessed that they belonged to the crew he had seen riding home from Cochimi.

It struck him as strange that the noise of the wagon didn't bring out any of the men. Tying the lines, he climbed down off the wagon and hailed, "Hello, the house!"

Nobody answered his greeting. He stood and listened. Nothing broke the hush that hung over the place. He glanced up at Susan on the wagon seat. She was turning her head uneasily this way and that. Her obvious distrust of the strange stillness increased rapidly, and communicated itself to him, and gave rise to a feeling in him that they were watched by something secret and hostile. He started for the bunkhouse, noting as he went that the roan horse had pricked up its ears inquisitively and was sniffing the air.

He was almost at the bunkhouse when a small sound stopped him, and he spun around, his right hand by instinct dropping to his holster. Susan cried a startled, "Jim!" to him. She twisted on the wagon seat and groped frantically inside the wagon.

A man wearing a green shirt stood in the open doorway of the blacksmith shed, gun in hand. He fired before Jim drew, and without waiting to see the result he sprinted to the wagon. Susan was dragging forth her father's rifle. With one swipe he knocked it from her hands. Men came running from behind the bunkhouse, Tillander and the deputy sheriff among them.

"Couldn't you wait?" demanded the deputy sheriff.

"No." The man in the green shirt picked up the silver-mounted rifle. He motioned with it at Jim Carmack, sprawled face down on the ground. "I never yet waited for anybody to do my killing."

Tillander smiled at Susan. "Welcome home!" he said softly.

Five

THE NIGHT BREEZE across Piedras Gordas was not too chill for comfort as long as a man kept his coat on, and although the moon was dipping low it yet shed light enough for easy travel on a clear road. Gently and steadily ascending, the road ran almost straight, having nothing but rocks to avoid. Later it would wind like a snake in and out and up the Santa Cruz to the diggings, as any mountain road had to do, forcing vigilance upon the traveler by night, but at this unobstructed level it made for monotony that, together with the moonlight and solitariness, encouraged meditation.

Gold, Lew Reagan mused, was invariably found in the most awkward places to get at, like most good things. Which seemed to indicate that, while man might be granted a right to pursue happiness, fate ensured that he didn't have any soft chase catching it. A man stubbed his toe so often, he got to where he couldn't even limp. Reagan worked his toes in his boots, thinking of Susan Harby: her eyes, her hair, lips . . .

At the back of his mind, detached from the present, lay a shelved thought of the rider who had passed him earlier in the night. The rider, coming up at a dead run within fifty yards of him, had shied off and quit the road, gone clattering wide around through the rocks and raced on. Wore something bundled over him like a blanket. An Indian, perhaps, scared of the dark. More likely some poor devil on the *cuidado*, new to the game, distrusting everybody, like Carmack when he was floundering in the Gila. The new ones always got disillusioned in mankind and saw enemies in every shadow, before experience taught them better.

Susan would marry Jim Carmack, and they'd raise a brood of kids and live moderately useful lives. Humdrum. She'd forget about a red dress and her being mistaken for a fancy woman in it, and about a man who once looked into her young eyes until she nearly obeyed his silent command to let down her defenses and come to him. Dishpans and diapers would roughen her hands, her soft skin would harden in the dry climate, and in a few years she'd look about the same as most ranchwomen. A trip to town every couple of

41

weeks; buy supplies, chat with neighbors, and home again, her husband worrying over bills and the current crop of calves. As exciting as a plate of beans. Without chili.

"Well, if that's what she wants..."

The black horse blew its nostrils gently. Reagan, acquainted with the animal's sharp senses, dropped his musings and brought full attention to the present. He was coming up a slight rise of the road, the ground bare about him on both sides, the nearest rock showing its top on the other side of the rise. His horse snorted more loudly. It hadn't the habit of nickering, for it happened not to be of a sociable disposition, but the snort told him that it sensed the presence of another horse somewhere in the near vicinity. He thought at once of the rider who had passed him hours ago.

"Resting ahead?" he muttered.

It wouldn't do to startle anyone so shy of strangers by coming upon him suddenly. Might shoot. On the other hand, unless he was fast asleep the man must have heard the black's hoofbeats and its snort, sounds that carried in the quiet night. He was probably sheltering among the rocks ahead, huddled in his blanket or whatever it was, within a jump of his horse. No campfire, no smell of one. Better to ride around him, discreetly, since privacy was his evident desire. Reagan reined the black over to leave the road, and as he did so the top of the tall rocks winked a flash.

The shot shook up his horse, the bullet went *phut!* past his face, and instantly he jabbed spurs and leaned into the wind. He rode at a tangent across the bald space, trying to keep himself below the level of the rise, and called out angrily, "Drop it, you crazy damned—"

The second shot zipped close overhead, and a third struck the top of the rise like a tiny explosion and droned off. The shooter was handling a repeater rifle fast, and he wasn't firing as a warning to stay clear. He had posted himself up on that rock to guard the road, fired to kill, and missed only because his target had made to move off the road before topping the rise, causing him to hurry his first shot. At that, it had been close.

"Hell! Was he waiting for me?" Reagan rode a wide half-circle as he had intended to do, putting himself beyond the rise and the tall rock, but there he drew in to stare back. The moon was meeting the horizon, silvering the tips of scattered rocks and outlining the one where the shooter had lain waiting.

The spot was well chosen for an ambush, by day or night,

42

and Reagan grew surer that the man had deliberately way-laid him. It made him coldly furious. He slid his rifle from its saddle boot and dismounted. His change of location gave him an even break now, for the man couldn't see him, although no doubt he had kept track of him by the sounds of the horse.

The tall rock, black against the moon, bulged at the bottom. Reagan took aim with his rifle. The bulge moved, and he fired. A horse screamed. On the instant a shot lashed at him, not from that rock but from another, closer in. It was aimed at his muzzle flash, and the bullet whipped up a rattle of echoes until it hit something behind him. There was some muffled noise of kicking, of creaking leathers, then those sounds ceased.

"Coming right after me, is he?" It confirmed Reagan in his certainty that the man had set himself to do a killing. The man was stalking him. Failing in his first attempt, he was determined to go through with it. He had to now, his horse dead and no course left for him to back out of and get away. Necessity made him more dangerous than ever.

The moon touched the horizon, seemed to hesitate, and sank out of sight. Reagan knew that he had to shift. He couldn't linger here out of cover. This had become a stalking match in the darkness, a deadly contest demanding silent movement. He dropped to all fours and peered low along the ground, but now that the moon was gone the scattered rocks were jumbled blurs in positions he had not had time to mark and memorize.

He hated leaving his horse standing on bare ground. Its noise would betray him and bring rapid fire from the repeater. The man wasn't apt to shoot the horse, though, if and when he got close enough to spot it. He'd be a fool to do that and leave them both afoot. Steal it, perhaps, or try, but not kill it.

"One of us will need it." Reagan murmured. "One of us . . ."

It occurred to him that the horse might be what the man was after. His mount could have caved in under the punishing rate he had ridden it earlier in the night, and he had to get another. There had to be a reason for his murderous ambush. That one was at least logical.

"If that's the case . . ." Reagan crawled off to the right, found a rock, and crouched against it. "If that's the case we'll let him try. Give him time."

From here he could make out the black shape of his

43

horse, standing quietly alone on the bare patch of earth, reins grounded. He settled down to wait for the next move. The horse was the bait. Whether or not possession of it had inspired the attack, it was a potent lure now that the man's mount was dead. A move of some kind had to come soon, for morning was not far off.

The cool night breeze, which Reagan had found bearable while riding, penetrated his clothes. Before long he was chilled, and because patient waiting was not his long suit he began questioning his decision to wait the man out. He heard not the slightest sound from him. Some grayness seeped up into the eastern sky, the horse stood out a little clearer, and nothing happened. Irritably he broke his motionless pose to ease a cigar from his pocket and chew on its end. A shot promptly cut off the brief moment of slackness.

It caught him unready, and the bullet, spanging off rock and whipping chips into his face, drove him back from his crouching squat so that he lost balance and landed on his shoulders with his rifle pointed skyward. Two more shots cracked. He rolled back to the cover of the rock, half blinded, cursing. That shooter had cat eyes and a cat's talent for stealthy prowling, and he hadn't fallen for the bait. He had crept around and outwaited his quarry. A patient devil. And where was he now?

Reagan wiped his eyes. There was a horrible taste in his throat. He coughed up a bit of cigar, spat it out, and a voice called mockingly, "Chest, Reagan? Too bad. Oughta gone lower!"

Knows me. Reagan mulled it over; the voice had no place in his memory. Thinks he's hit me. Thinks I'm coughing up blood. Got a glimpse of me, fired on spec, heard me spill like a fool on my back. He's not far away. But who is he?

He edged on around the rock. His rifle didn't please him for short-range shooting, and he laid it down and drew his right-hand gun crosswise from its holster, cocking it and muffling the click under his coat. Then he picked up the rifle and threw it forward. It fell in the dirt, making a hard thud that was difficult to identify.

The man fired immediately at the sound. He was a cloaked shape between two rocks when Reagan lunged out. Reagan snapped a shot, and it swayed and the repeater wavered. The second shot brought the shape tumbling down. Reagan stood for a minute and walked forward. "Enough?" he asked, but got no reply.

The man lay bundled in a long and heavy topcoat, an

44

English coachman's coat with shoulder cape attached. It had equipped him against the chill of night, and he must have borrowed it in a hurry, because all he wore under it were a thin silk shirt, bright green, and Levi pants. Reagan struck a match and stared down at the green shirt and at the face. This man had been one of the three who waylaid the Harby wagon in the Gila; their leader. There was no mistaking him.

The match burned down. Reagan flipped it away and sat pondering. Why had this man set an ambush for him with so much care and trouble? Revenge? That was the obvious answer—but how had he known which route to take? According to Frank Tillander, there were several routes to the Santa Cruz diggings. He had advised taking this one.

"Frank's the only one who knew," Reagan said aloud. "This feller didn't. He couldn't even know where I was going, unless Frank told him. Um!" He didn't take it kindly of Frank to steer this killer onto his trail, but after all, Frank had forty thousand dollars to think of, and he, Reagan, had put a bug in his ear. And, as Frank said, they had never pretended to be close friends.

He shook his head slowly. On further thought the motive lacked strength. Whatever Frank Tillander had gained from the murder of Amiel Harby, it was all his. Nobody could force him to disgorge any part of it, and he knew it. Yet he had tipped off this killer, a man who had no motive other than to pay off a grudge. There was something else behind the ambush.

Reagan took out a fresh cigar and a match, and as he lit the cigar his eyes were attracted by a shine of silver. The dead man lay on his rifle, his topcoat covering the barrel and breech, leaving the end of the butt exposed. Reagan stooped over and pulled it free, and shock held him motionless. It was a new Henry repeater, silver-mounted and engraved. Allen Harby's rifle. He would have recognized it in any collection anywhere, if only by the elaborate silver plate set into the butt. The last time he had seen it Susan Harby was holding it trained on him.

A pretty firearm, expensive, guaranteed to tempt such a man as this to steal it. Or, taking it by force, to keep it. Susan would hardly have parted with it willingly.

Reagan carried the rifle to his horse. He tightened cinch, legged up into the saddle, and rode northward. After its cooling wait the horse wanted to stretch out in a run, but he held it down to conserve it for the full journey back to Cochimi.

If Susan Harby had met with bad trouble, he was already too late to stand it off for her. Much too late.

Along the main street a constant opening and slamming of doors released snatches of music that tinkled through a roar of voices, and men tramped the boardwalks from place to place seeking new entertainments. One of a group of drunken riders emptied his gun in the air, squawling like an Apache. Maintaining its recently acquired reputation as a wide-open town that blossomed after dark, Cochimi was forging into its nightly frolic.

The blue wagon, minus its team, stood in front of the deputy sheriff's office and town jail.

Although Reagan had felt that Susan Harby must have come to grief, the presence of the wagon here was a mute corroboration that made his scalp prickle. His lips curled inward and he snarled silently at the deputy sheriff's office. There was no light in there. He guessed that the deputy was making his evening rounds. A look inside the wagon informed him that it was empty except for a few odds and ends. The deputy, then, had impounded the wagon and stripped it of all the Harby belongings. And what had he done with Susan?

"I'll kill him!" Reagan muttered.

At the livery, where he put up his horse, he saw the wagon team in the yard. He would have asked questions, but the stableman was surly, recognizing him as the trouble-some stranger who had disturbed his early-morning slumbers two days ago. Coming out, Reagan chose for his first call the Hi Jolly, remembering that the man in the green shirt had seemed to have some kind of connection with it, and at any rate he had emerged from it with others during that morning disturbance.

He pushed into the crowded barroom of the Hi Jolly and looked around carefully while elbowing a place for himself at the bar. There was a dance floor at one end, gambling tables at the other, and the hotel section upstairs was reached by a door marked "Rooms." The deputy was not present, nor anyone else he knew by sight, yet several men paid him second looks that were sharply quizzical. A bartender caught his signal and slid bottle and glass to him over the wet bar.

He took his first drink at a gulp and refilled the glass. A sign proclaimed that all drinks were fifty cents. Pretty steep even for a boom town, he considered. He put a five-dollar

46

bill on the bar. Nursing his second drink along with a cigar, he became aware of a pool of silence spreading around him. Men nearest him at the bar began drifting away. He smoked, outwardly abstracted, his ears attuned to an undertone of muttering. In the back-bar mirrors he could see men watching him, studying him frowningly as if not quite certain what to make of him, and he wondered about them. Soon one of them would brace him and then the others would come in on the play.

"Better get out of here." he told himself. But his mood was to stay and see it through. He lingered on.

Minutes passed. The bartender came to collect for the two drinks and brought his change, three cart wheels and a dollar bill, which he slapped deliberately into a puddle of beer. He was fat and short-legged, and had the face of a weary old cynic, yet he looked at Reagan with a kind of challenge in his eyes. Some of the watching men showed alert interest that lasted until the bartender moved away. The piano on the dance floor gave out a thumping rhythm, but no women appeared.

Reagan gathered up the three coins, idly jingling them, meditating on the bartender's act. If it was meant to prick his temper, why hadn't it been followed through when it failed? He turned the dollar bill over to wipe the beer off it. Scrawled on it with a blunt pencil was a single word: *Upstairs.*

The bartender was serving drinks halfway down the bar. Reagan wiped the dollar bill with his hand and turned it back over. A trap? Surely it was too clumsy. Yet such a terse message, or warning, might be calculated to succeed by its very obviousness, where something more subtle could fail. He thought it over. If the watching men had made up their minds to get him, their chance was right here and now. They didn't need to lure him upstairs.

He called down the bar, "Got a room for me?"

By the lull in the talk he knew that he was doing an unexpected thing. The bartender grunted. "Guesso," and stumped to the key rack. He threw a key down and snapped up the dollar bill in exchange. "Room Four suit you?"

"If it's got a bed."

"They all got beds. Three dollars. This'n's on the key, if you ever return it."

Reagan paid him back the three cart wheels and left the bar. The door with the "Rooms" sign had three wooden steps below it, and when he opened it he half turned. From

47

here he commanded a view of the entire barroom. The same men were watching him, making no attempt to disguise their watching. He let his eyes travel to the bar. The bartender had not asked him his name, although a register book hung alongside the key rack. He called, "My name's Reagan."

In the midst of washing glasses the bartender raised his head. He sent a glance over the men before leveling it at Reagan. "We know," he said.

Reagan let the door swing shut behind him. He was in a short hallway. a closed passage lighted dimly by a small lamp hung high on the wall. The other wall was taken up by the staircase that led to the upper floor. He climbed the stairs quietly, drawing a gun. He couldn't tell whether the bartender's parting words constituted a warning or a threat. The man was enigmatic. Almost certainly it was he who had scrawled the cryptic message on the dollar bill. Why he had done so was the puzzle. Room Four, perhaps, contained the answer.

Six

THE ROOM WAS empty. It was the second room from the head of the stairs, one of a dozen lining both sides of a narrow corridor, and the door stood wide open for Reagan's inspection. A wall lamp, like the one downstairs, was burning to show him an eight-by-ten crib that contained a bed and nothing else. There was one small window with the shade drawn. The air smelled stale and scented.

He closed the door, leaving it unlocked, and sat on the bed. While waiting, listening for sounds outside in the corridor, he puffed hard on his cigar to change the scent of the air. When presently a soft tread reached his ears, he did not rise. The door knob twisted noiselessly. He held the drawn gun between his knees and sat a little straighter. The door opened swiftly.

He rose and looked at Felisa Plevin. She, motioning to him for silence, closed the door with care and placed her ear to it. Satisfied after a long moment, she faced him. She was richly dressed, overdressed, as she had been when he met her riding in the buggy with Frank Tillander, but he saw now that she was not so Spanish as he had thought her then. Nor as young. She wore heavy make-up, and brought in with her a waft of perfume that practically nullified his cigar smoke.

"I've got to talk to you," she whispered. "Shorty—"

"The bartender?"

"He'll let us know if they start up. He's my friend."

That closed one question and opened others. "What's their grudge against me?" Reagan asked her.

"You should ask!" she retorted impatiently. "Didn't you kill Bo Conlan? Somewhere up in the Gila Country? Shanty Green saw you. He recognized you when you came through town a couple days ago."

"Shanty Green? Wore a green shirt?"

"Sure. He always wears green. Bo was his cousin. And the bunch liked him. That's grudge enough for them—even without Frank."

"Was Shanty Green working for Frank?"

She pulled her lips into a half smile. "You don't seem to

49

know what you've got into. That's funny. Frank thinks ...
Or are you trying to fool me, like all men?"

"No, Mrs. Plevin," Reagan said, "I'm not. Frank wasn't
much more than a tinhorn when I knew him. He had style,
and a fast way with women, but—"

"He's a big man now!" she interrupted. "Cattle and mining
interests. And he owns this place. I," she added with pride
and a note of bitterness, "helped him get his start. My late
husband left me some money."

Reagan, mindful of Frank Tillander's ways with women,
wondered briefly how the late Mr. Plevin had died. What
he wanted most to know was what had become of Susan
Harby, but he felt it best to lead the widow up to it by
degrees. She was devious and secretive, despite a surface
of frankness, likely to take refuge behind a weave of lies
if pressed too suddenly. "Is Frank afraid I'd blackmail him?"
he asked her. "About Harby?"

Felisa Plevin scanned his face critically. "It's more than
that, Mr. Reagan. It's the Harby girl. You're her—friend,
shall we say?"

"Let's say that."

"All right." She seated herself on the edge of the bed and
arranged her velvet skirt with a touch of coquetry that
Reagan guessed came as naturally to her as breathing. "You
fought for her and killed Bo, you and that cowpoke. You
rode in ahead of the wagon, on the scout, and gave Frank
the shock of his life. He knew about the fight, from Shanty
Green, and about the big joker on a black nag—but he didn't
know that was you. Had no idea until you showed up on
the road, with a bullet-cut hand, riding the black nag. Shock?
You can imagine!"

Reagan nodded, fitting facts and surmises together in his
mind. Frank Tillander had found out when the Harby
wagon was coming. He had posted a man up in Ute to
misdirect Allen Harby into the desert, and sent Shanty
Green with two others to make sure that it never got out.
"There's a lawyer here who wrote to Harby's brother, Allen,
telling him Harby was dead and had left him his property."

"Old Jeff Oakes. Meddling old drunk. Somebody spiked
his bottle, and he died."

"And Frank got his mail, eh? Frank went to considerable
trouble to keep that wagon from getting here, Mrs. Plevin!"

Her full dark eyes lifted obliquely to his. "He's climbed
high here. The higher you climb, the more trouble it takes
to protect yourself. Harby's brother was coming to claim

50

the Rocking H. Frank owns it. He holds a bill of sale, signed by Harby."

Reagan dropped the stub of his cigar on the floor and stepped on it. While not shatteringly surprised by the revelation, he needed a little time to get a grip on himself. He said, "And the bill of sale wouldn't stand up under inspection, of course, because it's a fake! You're being very open with me, Mrs. Plevin. I'm wondering why."

"I have a reason. A woman's best reason. The cowpoke and your little friend, the Harby girl, met a posse yesterday out at the Rocking H. Shanty Green shot the cowpoke. Frank grabbed the girl. Damn him, he's..."

Felisa Plevin paused to listen to a rise of noise from the barroom downstairs, and Reagan asked through his teeth, "Then what?"

"Wait a minute!" She held up her fingers, listening further. "Frank's come in!" The noise subdued, and she bit her lower lip nervously. "He knows now you're here!"

"Tell me what happened at Rocking H!"

"Heckels was there. Our deputy sheriff. He's Frank's man, sort of, but as I hear it he stood up to him that time. The cowpoke was still breathing, and they wanted to finish him off. Heckels wouldn't have it. He arrested him and put him in the wagon, and there was another argument over—"

"To hell with Carmack!" Reagan cut in. "What happened to the girl?"

"I'm telling you!" Felisa Plevin snapped. "The upshot was, Heckels arrested her, too. He charged them both with possession of a stolen horse and suspicion of murder. Frank was furious. He'd have shot Heckels, I guess, only he can't afford to—he'd have the district sheriff on him. Frank has other ways, though, of getting at a man. Heckels' nerve was dragging low by the time he reached town with his two prisoners. They let him jail the cowpoke, but as for the girl ...Frank said that as a private citizen he wouldn't let any girl be locked up in a stinking jail, no matter what she was or what she'd done. Oh, he was self-righteous! Heckels finally broke down and released the girl into Frank's personal and protective custody."

"Where is she?"

"I snatched her away from Frank and put her under *my* personal custody!" The woman made a savage little sound in her throat. "I've given everything to Frank—everything! But he's gone mad over this girl. I think he might even marry her to keep the Harby ranch, if I don't put a stop to it. I've got her locked up here in one of the rooms."

She rose to her feet as Reagan turned to the door. "Not so fast, Mr. Reagan! This is a bargain between us, not a free ticket for you to do as you please!" She held a pistol in her hand, a little two-shot derringer, large in its capacity to do damage at five paces.

Reagan glanced at it and at her. He had small sympathy to spare for the woman, who plainly did not look for any. She was following the dictates of self-interest, and in protecting Susan she was only trying to save herself from discard. It was a foredoomed effort on her part, for Frank Tillander never kept his women long, and when he was through with them he made it brutally final.

She said over the pistol, "Anything can happen in this place. Frank's given it out that the Harby girl's an imposter, a Lulu who's been using a false name, knocking around with a horse thief. She could scream bloody murder, and folks will only think she's drunk and cutting up. How long can I hold Frank in line?"

"No longer than suits him. No woman ever did."

Her eyes narrowed at the thrust. "She's yours! Get her out of here! I'll help you any way I can. I don't know how you'll do it, and I don't care—but get her out! Get her to hell out of Frank's reach!"

He put his hand on the doorknob. "Let's go."

"You're not to kill Frank!" she whispered. "No matter what happens, you're not to kill him! Or I'll kill her!"

"Is that part of our bargain?"

"Yes—and you'd better keep to it!"

He nodded, and said again, "Let's go."

She brushed by and preceded him along the corridor. The barroom beneath gave up only a low hum of voices, and she walked on tiptoe, Reagan matching her stealth. Coming to the last door at the end of the corridor, she fitted a key noiselessly into the lock and swung it inward, and when a hinge creaked she hissed as though it had been an explosion.

The room was exactly like the one they had left. Same size, same minimum of furnishings. It smelled much the same, too.

Susan Harby sprang up off the bed at sight of Reagan. She was fully dressed, but he thought perhaps that had she not been she might still have given way to that impulse, she was manifestly so overjoyed to see him. She rushed to him, and the next instant he had her in his arms.

"Lew Reagan! Oh, Lew, it's you—it's really you!" She pressed her face against the front of his shirt. "I knew you'd come back! I *knew* you would!"

"Quiet!" hissed Felisa Plevin urgently. To get the door shut, she had to shove at Reagan, and he lifted Susan in his arms and moved farther with her into the cramped little room.

It did no good for reason to tell him that all this unreserved gladness might well be the natural reaction of an overwrought girl. That she had come through a terrifying experience calculated to break down her courage. That on the lonely edge of her despair he had appeared, Lew Reagan; and that in her eyes at this moment Lew Reagan was a man without fault or blemish.

It did no good until she said, "Lew! Jim's hurt! They shot him! That horrible man in the green shirt . . ."

He silently bedamned Jim Carmack for his intrusion again at the worst possible time. He reached over Susan and turned down the wick of the wall lamp. He set Susan aside on her feet, stepped to the window, and raised the shade. He tried to open the window, and Felisa Plevin said, "These windows don't open. Anyway, it's too small for you to get through. Besides, Frank's got a man on watch down there in the side alley."

It gave him an excuse to swear aloud and he used it. "Then how do we get out of this perfumed piggery?" he demanded.

His rude term for the hotel aroused in Felisa Plevin a perverse loyalty toward it and an acid attitude toward him. Guests, she stated, used the stairs and went out through the barroom. There was no other exit. It was arranged purposely to foil deadbeats from skipping their bills. The problem it posed was Reagan's, not hers; she had already done more than her share.

She went on to say that she couldn't be expected to solve *every* little difficulty. Men were all alike. Wanted everything done for them, wanted waiting on hand and foot. Give any man an inch . . .

Susan sent Reagan a look of perfect confidence, a look that said she was safe in his care and couldn't possibly come to harm with him on hand.

Between them Reagan felt fractured, half inferior and half godlike. Women. To their judgment a man was either nothing or was everything. Wrong on both counts, still they calmly loaded onto him tasks that would baffle a gaggle of witches.

He looked at Susan. His arms knew the slimness of her waist, and he ran a measuring eye over her build. Susan colored. Reagan looked at the window and estimated that she would be able to wriggle through it when the pane was smashed out. "Tear up those bedcovers and make a rope," he instructed her. "You'll have to break the window and climb down outside."

Felisa Plevin whispered an objection. "They'll hear it!"

"Not if there's enough noise in the barroom to cover it."

"How about the man on watch in the alley?"

"After the noise starts, give him a minute to run round front. He's bound to be curious to see what the row's about. Then break the window," he told Susan, "and climb down fast. Pick a horse off the street and ride north. Stay on the stage road. Keep going."

"But where will you—"

"I'll be along sooner or later. You'll be all right." Of the two comforting predictions he thought that the second was likeliest to come true. She'd have a fair chance of catching up with a northbound stage to Ute, and once there the law would hear her story and look into it. "I've got to see about making a noise," he mentioned.

Felisa Plevin stepped with him to the door. "Frank's down below!"

"So you said."

"You're not to kill him!"

"You said that before, too."

"If you do ... !" She pointed her pistol at Susan. "You understand, Mr. Reagan?"

"I do, Mrs. Plevin," he murmured. "And I'd like to wring your neck!"

He closed the door, paced lightly along the corridor, and with a normal tread walked downstairs to the barroom.

Seven

FRANK TILLANDER SAT with three men at a round table on the edge of the dance floor. One of the three was a working cowman, by his garb, a man up in his forties. The other two were younger and had on engineer's boots, the kind worn by most company mining men above pick-and-shovel rank. With his left elbow on the table Frank was juggling a twenty-dollar gold piece, making it roll back and forth between his fingers as he talked. His three companions watched the flashing coin as if hypnotized.

The coin stilled, and Reagan, coming into the barroom, met a dead stare. Frank curled his fingers to him in a beckoning gesture. Reagan made his way to the table, noting that Shorty, the bartender, turned his back after one quick glance and busied himself at the back bar. Noting, too, that nearby tables were occupied by the men who had previously been watching him.

Frank wore tonight a frock coat of fine broadcloth and a white linen shirt. He looked as loose-jointed as ever, slumped in his chair, sidelong to the table, the knee of a crossed leg cocked high, yet a gangling elegance marked him apart from other men as expensively dressed—gold miners and professional gamblers, wearing diamonds. Evening brought out the cream of Cochimi and it clotted here in the Hi Jolly, evidently.

"Lew," he said blandly as Reagan stopped at the table, "this is Deck Floyd, my ranch foreman. And Bob and Pack Meddaugh, business associates of mine. Gentlemen—Longrider Reagan."

Reagan exchanged nods with them. He placed Deck Floyd as the type of foreman made for anybody like Frank. A knotty man with a tight face and marble eyes, the kind of man who would carry out any order and keep his mouth shut. The Meddaugh brothers, if they were brothers, were simply mining men, possibly high-graders or at least touched with larceny, else Frank wouldn't have them.

"Sit down, Lew." Frank Tillander began juggling the gold piece again, not looking at it. "Glad you came down. Want a talk with you."

As soon as Reagan reached for a chair, Deck Floyd and the Meddaughs scraped back theirs and stood up. They moved off without a word. "Cigar?" Frank asked.

"Got one."

The coin disappeared. Frank stretched out a lighted match and held it for Reagan. "Well, Lew?" he said.

"Well, Frank?" Reagan sucked in the flame, got an even burn, and expelled smoke. "You flimflammed me a little bit, you know. I figured you'd got Harby's money, of course. The money he rascalled us out of, I mean. That was all right. Hell with it. But you got his ranch, too, and that I don't like."

"The ranch was all there was," Frank said. "Harby blew the whole wad on it. Haven't you seen it?"

"Not yet."

"Oh?" The gold piece started its to-and-fro flipping. "I don't know what your game is, Lew. Not blackmail. Not your style. Anyway, I couldn't pay off. I'm spread out damned thin."

"You're living high and you meet a big payroll. The widow's money?"

"Felisa's money wasn't much. I used it up." Frank leaned forward confidentially. "This place isn't paid for yet. I have to use the profits as fast as they come in, to cover the Rocking H bills and my mining interests. The ranch won't begin paying off until I sell a beef herd. Then I'll be set. But right now I'm strapped for ready cash."

"You'll make out. You're on the upgrade. You'll end up the big kingpin of Cochimi. No, the big cattleman—that's what you always wanted, as I recall. Big cattleman. Respected. Hah!" Reagan spat out a flake of tobacco, remembering ambitions talked of four years ago over hidden campfires on the Texas border.

Shorty waddled out from behind the bar, obsequious, to inquire as to their wants. They waved him away. "Probably," Reagan observed matter-of-factly, "what you'll do, Frank, is stick up a gold shipment from the mines. You've got the right contacts, I guess." He looked at the Meddaughs, who had taken seats not far off. Then he looked at Frank Tillander, and saw from Frank's gaze that he had hit home. "Well, I be damned!" he exclaimed softly.

Frank said, "All right! You want in on it?"

"With you?" Reagan shook his head. "You just might put another Shanty Green onto me!"

"Shanty? I don't know—"

56

"He was waiting for me on the Piedras Gordas. He's dead."

"Tough," Frank said. He heaved his shoulders, sitting up. The twirling gold coin faltered, nested neatly between forefinger and thumb, and a springlike flick of the thumb catapulted it at Reagan's face. "You—"

With one knee Reagan tipped the table into Frank's fast-following draw. He lunged across the upended table, ramming it harder into Frank, and his hands found Frank's throat. His elbows clamped down on Frank's arms. The table was sandwiched flat between them, blocking them both from making gunplay. Deck Floyd, the Meddaughs, and men at nearby tables jumped up staring, momentarily confused.

Reagan changed his grip, sliding an arm around Frank's neck and hugging his head up close. He freed a gun and, poking it over Frank's shoulder at the men, he said, "Stay out of this!"

But he needed noise—noise to cover the smashing of the small window upstairs. Frank Tillander was struggling mightily to twist loose. Reagan brought back the butt of his gun and smacked him smartly above the ear with the heel of it. Frank sagged, and Reagan, using him and the table as his shield, worked backward toward the doors. He fired at a hanging bar lamp. The lamp shattered, burst into flame, and abruptly there was noise enough to drown out the breaking of a dozen windows.

Shorty ran out from the bar, hollering for help to put out the oil blaze. Some of the crowd responded by unhooking the nearest of half-a-dozen fire buckets that hung around the walls and dashing at the bar, while those standing at the bar backed hastily away from it, causing mix-ups. The blaze becoming the chief concern, men swarmed heedlessly between Reagan and the group he was trying to hold covered.

Deck Floyd shouted, "Damn you, Shorty, douse your own fire! Come on, fellers!"

The group split up, shoving through the milling crowd and making for Reagan. He let Frank Tillander fall and, spinning around in a crouch, he plunged at the doors. His head and shoulders knocked the doors wide apart on their spring hinges and, diving on out, he collided full force with a man who was coming in. For the moment he had forgotten about the man on watch in the side alley. His hurtling weight carried them both crashing to the boardwalk and on under the forefeet of the horses tied to the front hitch rack. The horses jerked back, whistling snorts. Four of them snapped their bridle reins and went bucking along the street.

The man should have had the breath driven out of him, but his reflexes were prompt and he was nimble. He squirmed clear of the tangle, kicking and beating at Reagan, and was scrambling upright when Reagan booted his legs from under him and brought him down again. He grunted, flopping over to clear his holster. With a long stroke Reagan connected the barrel of his gun with the man's jaw.

Reagan's hat had been jammed down on his ears by butting through the doors, and with no time to adjust it he had to tip his head up to see what was going on. The doors were still flapping. At each flap he glimpsed the faces of men coming out after him. He fired five times into the doors, getting to his feet. By now, he hoped, Susan was climbing down from the window. The dark mouth of the side alley was only a few steps from him. She ought to be emerging from it any second. He stayed where he was, exchanging his emptied gun for its loaded mate, to hold off Tillander's bunch and give Susan time to borrow a horse.

Somebody, a heavy man, came trotting purposefully down the street toward him. The deputy sheriff, he guessed. Cochimi didn't seem to have a town marshal. Heckels was all the law there was here. And he's not much to crow about! Reagan thought.

Susan didn't appear. A pistol shot cracked loudly in the side alley. He called sharply, "Susan!" When she still didn't appear, or answer him, he darted into the alley to look for her.

He found her lying in a crumpled heap beneath the second-floor window. The rope of bedcovers was being drawn upward. Its end disappeared through the broken window, and the window went dark. "Susan!" he whispered. "Susan . . ."

She didn't move.

The heavy footsteps of the deputy sheriff approached the mouth of the alley. Kneeling beside Susan in the darkness, Reagan leveled his gun ready, not caring now whom he shot down. But the deputy sheriff trotted on past the alley without a glance. He had a shotgun, and presently he was rapping questions to men swarming out of the barroom.

Reagan lifted Susan up in his arms and carried her on through the alley. Its rear end led to open back yards littered with rubbish. He stopped behind a pile of empty beer barrels to shift Susan onto his left shoulder, leaving his right hand and gun free for action. How badly she was hurt he couldn't tell. She was breathing, but limply unconscious. He spared a further moment there, listening to the onset of noise, the shouting and hurried tramping of men. They were on the hunt for him; Frank Tillander's men and the deputy. And Frank himself, if he'd recovered yet from that clout. And if Frank had discovered Susan's escape . . .

His mind raced, desperately seeking a chance. Susan needed a doctor, and Cochimi probably had one, but where to find him he didn't know. No hope now of lifting horses from a hitchrack, and the livery stable was down on the other side of the street. And no use to go trudging off cross-country on foot, without knowledge of the country, leaving it to luck to stumble on some place where he and Susan could take shelter.

He shook his head, scowling at the sounds of the searchers. Got to find a place to hole up in, somewhere not far off, for the time being. Some place where they wouldn't think of looking right away. Where, if they did, he could stand them off. Where maybe he could get in touch with a doctor. If not a doctor, well, he had helped patch up a few wounds himself. He'd have to do the best he could for Susan. A pocket derringer did hideous damage, though, when it struck the mark. The black-eyed witch had jumped to the conclusion that the barroom shooting meant that Frank was killed, and she had carried out her threat of reprisal.

He sighed, absently patting Susan. Some place—but where? He was asking too much. Stranger in a hostile country, with a hurt girl to take care of . . . "Settle for any damn' place at all," he muttered. "Any stinking hole . . ."

His own words inspired an idea. He rejected it as insanely hopeless. But then he saw men coming around the rear of the Hi Jolly, spreading out in organized search, some with lanterns. Ahead of them stalked Frank Tillander and the deputy. Frank was hatless and his stride was a trifle unsteady. He spoke to the deputy. The men paused alertly, guns raised, as the deputy shouted, "Come out, Reagan!"

Reagan crept off, bent low to avoid the sky line and covering Susan's dress as best he could with his dark coat. He couldn't keep this up long. The whole town would take up the hide-and-seek game before the night was over. There were always volunteers aplenty for a man hunt. He picked his way carefully uphill through the littered back yards, looking for the town jail.

The front window of the deputy sheriff's office was bare of any kind of shade, and it showed a light. Peering from the corner of the narrow building, Reagan observed the activity down along the lower part of the street. The searchers were going at it methodically, combing the town, sure that he was lying low somewhere in it. They hadn't yet reached this upper end, but they would soon.

He cursed the deputy's office lamp and the bare window. The light fanned out onto the blue wagon in front. Darkness was his only ally. No hiding place, the wagon. It had to be the jail, the stinking jail, last place they'd think of looking into, one the doctor could visit without question if there were some way to send for him, and the tighest place in town for a man to make a stand. Spare guns and ammunition in the deputy's office.

Susan stirred feebly. Reagan held her like a sleeping child, her head resting against the side of his neck, one arm hanging down his back and her legs partly across his middle. She had lost her shoes and her hair had come undone. His arm ached. He eased her weight farther onto his shoulder.

"Here goes . . . !"

He left the corner and hugged the wall to the office door. The deputy had not stopped to lock up when he hurried out. Reagan threw the door open and, shutting it behind him, he swept a quick survey over the office to impress its contents on his memory before blowing out the lamp. A battered desk and two chairs, a bunk with its blankets in careless disorder, sheafs of wanted-bills tacked on a wall, and a gun rack containing two rifles. Near the gun rack, on the floor, were the Harby belongings taken from the wagon. They looked as though they had been thoroughly ransacked.

A puff of breath into the glass chimney put the lamp out. He lowered Susan onto the bunk. She was regaining consciousness, and he, fearing that she might roll off the bunk, and feeling that she had already been joggled too much despite the care he had taken, warned her, "Don't move! Just lie there quiet. I'll get a doctor somehow."

He considered bolting the front door, but decided against it. There was another door at the back of the office, and he opened it, made out dimly a barred window, and shut it again. The jail. No need for it right at present. Later. He lifted the two rifles from the gun rack and checked them.

60

Both were loaded, and the shelf above held two boxes of shells.

"Where are you hit?" he asked Susan, but she only mumbled indistinctly.

He would have to know, but first there were other things to do, to prepare for what was bound to come. A drawer of the desk yielded three six-guns and a further supply of shells. He again asked Susan where she was hit, and she echoed vaguely, "Hit?"

She was making a little progress, anyway. It encouraged him to hope that her wound was not one beyond mending. In another drawer he found a bottle of whiskey, a water bottle, and a clean tumbler. A man of somewhat fussy personal habits, the deputy. Reagan mixed whiskey with water and took it to the bunk.

"Susan," he said, raising her head gently, "drink some of this. " And when she obediently sipped, he asked, "Where did Felisa shoot you?"

"I'm not—" she began, and coughed on the whiskey.

He drank the rest from the tumbler himself and reframed his question. "Where do you hurt most?"

"My head."

It wasn't her head. He didn't believe it for an instant. A derringer slug would have made a bloody mess of that pretty head. She wasn't telling him where she was hurt, because he was a man. Because, incredibly, of maidenly modesty, an insane squeamishness.

Well—he set the tumbler on the floor—he would find out for himself, then. Have to use firmness. Save her life, modesty or no modesty . . .

She pushed his exploring hands off pretty vigorously and sat up. "I'm not shot!" she stated distinctly. "I saw her lean out the window and point the pistol at me while I was climbing down, and I let go and fell. I must have stunned myself. Where are we?"

He picked up the tumbler, took it to the desk, sloshed straight whiskey into it, and drank with mingled emotions. He was vastly relieved for her sake, and hardly knew why he was mad at the same time, unless it was because he felt like a fool.

"Where are we?" she insisted, and he heard her groping around the bunk in the dark. "Where have you gone?" She sounded lost, reminding him that after all she had only just come out of a faint.

"I'm right here with you, in the deputy sheriff's den."

"You mean we're in jail, Lew? I thought—"

"Not yet! This is his office. The jail's in back."

"Is Jim there? Is he all right?"

"Jim? Oh—Carmack." Reagan listened to heavy footsteps outside. "I didn't ask. Quiet, now, somebody's coming! Don't make a sound!"

"I won't," she promised. The bunk creaked.

"Don't move!" The footsteps clumped on the short length of boardwalk fronting the office.

"I'm not," she whispered. "It's this thing I'm sitting on!"

"Sssssh!"

The door swung open and the pale rectangle framed the blocky figure of Depty Sheriff Heckels. "Hunh!" grunted the deputy. Leaving the door open, he came in, familiarity guiding him to the lamp. "Sworn I filled it yes'day." He put down his shotgun. A match scraped, flared alight.

The bunk creaked.

Eight

THE SOUND BROUGHT the deputy sheriff's head around. His bearded jaw dropped, but no words came from his mouth.

Sitting on the bunk, barefoot, with her hair all undone and her dress disheveled, Susan did not resemble anything like the result of a sheltered life. Even to Reagan, who knew better, she gave the appearance of beautiful abandon, of a lovely young profligate the worse for a wild night. The disordered bunk and the whiskey bottle completed the picture.

Heckels stood staring, dumfounded, his hands raised to the lamp, the match burning unheeded in his fingers, until Reagan pressed the muzzle of a gun to his spine. "Let go the match," Reagan murmured, "and keep your hands where they are!"

He reached around the deputy and lifted his gun from its holster. "Go shut the door! Bolt it. I can see pretty good in the dark, so don't do anything foolish." And after Heckels did as he was told. "Hang something over the window. Throw him a blanket, Susan."

The blanket, thrown blindly by Susan, brought a complaining grunt from Heckels. He clawed it away from his face and draped it folded over the front window. Reagan then lighted the lamp, turning the wick down low. Regaining a stolid composure, Heckels inquired dryly, "D'you reckon to get away?"

"Might, with some help from you," Reagan told him.

"Me?" Heckels tapped the badge pinned on his vest. "I'm a law officer."

Reagan nodded. "I'm not too partial to your breed in general. I particularly despise a law officer who sells out his badge."

Heckels flushed darkly. "Nobody could pay me to help a dodger and his—"

"The young lady is Miss Susan Harby," Reagan cut in sharply. "She's Amiel Harby's niece and holds legal claim to his property. Her father was Amiel's brother, Allen Harby, a schoolteacher from Colorado."

Susan spoke up. "I taught school too!"

Heckels shifted his eyes to her. "Frank Tillander says she's lying. Says she's an impostor and a . . . Well, fact is I don't find it hard to believe!"

"I made the same mistake at first," Reagan admitted. "It's something about her looks. She can't help that. Not her fault she's all woman. You should see her in a red dress!"

Susan rose hurriedly from the bunk, her face crimson. With prim gestures she arranged her dress and brushed back her hair. She marched straight to the rear door, opened it, and called, "Jim! Are you in there?" Jim Carmack's voice answered, "Susan!" and she ran on into the jail.

The deputy gazed wonderingly after her. "I never in my life saw any Lulu blush like that!" he said. "All of a sudden she looks different. Looks respectable and—well—moral!"

"She's as moral as—as . . ." Offhand, Reagan couldn't think of anybody as determinedly moral as Susan Harby. Through the open door to the cells he heard her saying, "Lew Reagan is here, Jim! He's come to get you out."

That was news to Reagan. He discounted it. Carmack had had his chance, bobbled it, and a set of iron bars between him and Susan seemed morally fitting. Furthermore, Carmack had let himself get shot by Shanty Green on the Rocking H. If he couldn't do better than that when he was well, injured he was a liability, one that Reagan felt no urge to shoulder. Carrying Susan was another matter entirely.

Heckels asked once more, "You reckon to get away?" But he put the question reasonably, without dryness. "Tillander's got enough men on his side to eat you! He can count on a dozen more!"

"Including you!"

"Not always. It was me brought Carmack and the girl in off the Rocking H, over Tillander's objections."

"So the Plevin woman told me. Why did you?"

Heckels went behind his desk and lowered himself into his chair. He said slowly, "I was appointed deputy here a good many years ago. I've served under five district sheriffs. They kept me on because I belong here, because it's my part o' the country. Everybody in it knew me. The cattle folks, I mean, and the old town folks. Things went along pretty quiet on the whole. A few upsets. Sat'day nights. Young cowpokes cutting up. Nothing serious. A woman, any woman, could go anywhere, any time, and every man lifted his hat to her. You could leave anything you owned anywhere, and it'd still be there when you got back."

Reagan shifted impatiently, saying, "I didn't ask you for the history of Cochimi!"

"What's your hurry? You ain't going anywhere! Tillander's got the town covered." The deputy resumed his monologue. "It's all changed since the mines opened up. Nearly everybody heading for the Santa Cruz comes through here. They outfit here and go on. If they make any money, they come back here to spend it. If they go broke, they come back here on the mooch—or on the prowl. Drifters, tramps, tinhorns, the usual scum. Hardcases. Gunmen. The town's full of 'em! They'd kill a man for the price of a drink! A decent woman daren't show her face in the street! They'd insult her in broad daylight! That's how bad it is!"

He slapped the desk top softly with the flat of his hand. "What can one man do? I've asked for help. It don't come. The cattle folks are disgusted, but they tolerate it, and that don't help me, either. They don't have to live with it. They come in as usual, grumble over high prices and the sorry state of the town, and go back home. Tillander's the only man with any control over the riffraff. The best I can do is play along with him, more or less, if I'm to keep some kind of order. I don't know why I'm telling you this."

"Trying to justify yourself?" Reagan suggested bluntly. "If you can't beat 'em, join 'em! That's what you've done, isn't it?"

"Damn it, no! I use Tillander to—"

"You? He's got a ghost cord tied to your nose, and any time he twitches it hard enough you quit bucking! You're scared of him, just plain scared, or you wouldn't be trying to justify yourself with this pious gab about using him to help you run the town. *He's* running the town! He's your boss!"

The deputy angrily started up from his chair and sank back again. A dead calmness settled over his face. He said, "If *you* think that, God knows how many more think the same!"

Reagan shrugged indifferently. "It may be the reason why you don't get better help. Cowmen aren't blind, whatever else they are. You may have been a middling-honest lawman once, but you're Frank Tillander's man now!" He pointed a toe at the pile of Harby belongings on the floor. "Was it you searched this stuff?"

"No. Somebody went through it before I got around to lugging it here."

"That would be Frank. You can bet he destroyed any proof he found that Susan is Harby's niece."

"You're guessing. How d'you know?"

65

"How do I know it's a wolf when it howls? Frank holds the Rocking H on a fake bill of sale that he knows is too shaky to stand challenging. He sent Shanty Green and two others to stop the Harby wagon from getting here. They killed Susan's father. About that time I got into it. And Carmack. Frank's got a special reason for wanting to hang onto that ranch. A handy remount station for a gang taking a flyer at the Santa Cruz gold shipments!"

Heckels shook his head. "You're wrong there. I reckon you haven't seen that ranch yet. It's a beaut. Frank thinks the world of it. He's got big plans for building it up and making it the finest outfit in the valley. What he wants worse than anything is for the cow folks all to look up to him. That's why he never treads on their toes if he can help it."

So, Reagan mused, Frank Tillander was bitten by that old bug, the itch for respectability and prestige. He could understand it, having been bitten by it himself. The belated ambition of drifters. A man went along, with his hat his only permanent roof, free of ties, rootless and uncaring for years, and suddenly something awakened a discontent in him. A hankering replaced the old contempt for stability, and any rancher became an aristocrat to be envied. It was a fairly predictable malady and generally came too late for any cure.

But who would have thought that Frank would get the craving to be a respected cattleman? Frank Tillander, with his fly-by-night ways, his women, his fondness for easy money and expensive dissipation, and his scorn of anything resembling a settled life. Yet he was already within reach of his goal, the lucky dog. No, not lucky. Smart. A smart cutthroat. Knew where he was going, and bent everything to his purpose.

"Maybe I should take lessons from him!" Reagan muttered wryly, and Heckels said, "What?"

"Nothing. Just thinking out loud. No I haven't seen the Rocking H. It must be pretty good, if Frank's building his whole future on it."

"It will be." Heckels watched Reagan's face curiously. "I gather he'll sell the Hi Jolly and his mining interests, and put the money into more cattle and land. Naturally, he don't want bad neighbors. Harby, now, he didn't make himself popular. Not friendly, and didn't like callers. Nobody missed him much when he got shot."

"Frank didn't miss him!"

"How'd you mean that?"

Reagan rolled a shoulder, not replying, and stepped to the open door of the jail. He was tired of the deputy sheriff's stubborn denseness. He tried to listen to what Susan and Carmack were saying, but their voices were only a murmur. Susan was a dim figure outside cell bars, and Carmack was a vague blur inside. Reagan turned back restlessly, to see Heckels sliding open a drawer.

"I took the guns out of your desk, Heckels!"

"So I see!"

"But not the handcuffs. Get 'em out, and give me your keys!"

His mood was ungentle as he manacled the deputy sheriff with his own handcuffs and took possession of his ring of assorted keys.

Heckels protested that he had only been getting at his pipe and tobacco, and that he'd had no idea of grabbing for a gun, but Reagan ordered him to be quiet. He didn't trust an obstinate man, least of all a mule-headed lawman who probably considered himself something pretty special with a gun.

Susan had heard Reagan speak of keys, for she came into the office, took them from his hand, said, "Thank you," and darted back into the jail before Reagan could think of any good reason to stop her.

A cell door clanged. Heckels showed by his reaction that he was perhaps not so mulish as he had appeared to be. The freeing of the prisoner didn't bother him. He actually grinned at Reagan's expression. His grin was understanding, edged with man-to-man mockery. "This gets interesting!" he observed, and Reagan saw him for the first time as a person, an individual, not as a somewhat dull type of middle-aged lawman embittered by his thankless job.

"Go to blazes!" Reagan growled, and the deputy's ironic grin deepened.

Susan and Carmack came in from the jail. Jim Carmack had a bandaged head and he was more hollow-eyed than before, but his voice rang a desperately confident note when he spoke. "Hello, Reagan! Thanks for the lift? Got horses?" He laid a hand on Susan's shoulder. "Have to make sure she gets away safe. Where's my gun, Heckels?"

Reagan eyed him somberly for a moment, then his temper slipped. "No horses," he said softly, "and the town's covered. But don't let any trifles like thirty or forty men cramp your style, hero!"

Jim Carmack, brought up short, exclaimed, "What?"

"We only need you to mow 'em down, hero!" Reagan' tone roughened. "I'll just sort of limp along behind, keepin score!"

"Now look, Reagan—"

"I'm looking, Carmack! I'm looking at the ten-thumbe tramp who dropped his deck, let Susan in for this jackpot and comes prancing in now like Fetterman at Fort Kearny Here's your gun, and another to go with it. Rifles there in the corner. Don't shoot your foot off—you'll want it to pu in your mouth!"

Jim caught the two guns that Reagan threw to him. " admit I didn't show so good," he said levelly. "Bad luck. I wasn't looking for any trouble on the Rocking H. But I'm not trying to—"

"Luck!" Reagan snorted. He knew how a streak of bad luck could defeat the best of men, but he had the urge to belittle Jim Carmack in Susan's eyes. "I can see why the losing end seems to be your natural place! Anybody with you on his side is a dead duck!"

Jim's anger flared. "Say what you mean, bad man!"

"You're a hoodoo!"

"To you, you mean!"

"This," Heckels repeated, "gets interesting!" Hurried foot-steps beat on the boardwalk outside. "I only came back to get my handcuffs for Frank. He wanted we should put 'em on Miss Harby, to keep her safe out of mischief while this commotion was going on. He didn't know she'd already skipped." Somebody tried the front door. "That's Frank now," said Heckels, rising.

Banging on the door, Frank Tillander called through it savagely, "Open up, Heckels! The girl's gone from her room! Reagan's got her! He choked Felisa senseless and . . ." The banging stopped. "Heckels! What are you locked in for? Open the door!"

Heckels, his wrists handcuffed behind him, looked inquiringly at Reagan. Jim Carmack blew out the lamp.

Frank Tillander shouted down the street, "Come and break this door in. Something wrong here!"

Reagan whispered to Susan, "Give me the keys, quick!"

"I left them in the cell door! I'll get them . . ."

There was no time for that. Some of Tillander's searching men could be heard running up the street. The deputy sheriff would have to be forced to play his part while handcuffed. Reagan pushed him to the door. He slid the bolt, gave the

68

door a pull, and stepped aside as it swung open. His gun was leveled at Heckels, who stood unmoving in the dim light that entered from the street.

Frank Tillander peered in at the deputy. "What the devil's the matter with you, Heckels?" he demanded. "Why didn't you answer me?" Then, detecting the wrongness of the deputy's silence and odd posture of hands behind the back, he made to retreat a step.

Reagan, moving forward and changing the aim of his gun, said, "Come in, Frank!" He watched the pale face go frozen, watched Frank Tillander fling a glance to the men coming up the street, and he said, "Come in alive, or stay out dead!"

Nine

TILLANDER CAME IN, Heckels stepping back to give him room to pass, and Reagan held his gun on him while he closed the door and fastened it. With the window covered it was pitch dark in the office. The darkness gave risk that Tillander might draw a pistol and turn the situation into a blindman's buff duel. "Light the lamp, Carmack," Reagan said.

Jim Carmack was striking a match before the words were out, but Reagan had to add, "If you can do it without setting fire to the place!"

With the lamp relighted Reagan looked at Tillander. "Glad you dropped by, Frank, we can use you! Search for his gun, Carmack, and don't forget his sleeves!"

Reaching the deputy's office and finding the door shut, the men were talking puzzledly together outside. Tillander stood quietly while Jim Carmack searched him. He gazed about him, settling his eyes last on Susan as she entered with the deputy's keys. "Use me, Lew? How?"

"Hostage," Reagan said.

Tillander smiled faintly, apparently unruffled and at ease, not removing his gaze from Susan. "Now, Lew!" he murmured chidingly. "You and I know of men who pulled some amazing getaways. Kidnaping a hostage never helped any of them! In the long run a hostage slows up the getaway and gives steam to the chase. You know it as well as I do. Nobody loves a kidnaper."

Reagan acknowledged the truth of it by making no retort, but Jim Carmack said, "You kidnaped Susan Harby!"

Tillander glanced at him. "The young woman was placed in my custody by a duly appointed officer of the law. As for her being Susan Harby, that's for her to prove. We all know she's nothing but a—"

"Don't say it, or I'll slam your teeth in!" Jim warned him. "You know it's a lie, as well as I do! She had the proof until you stole it, you crook!"

Tillander looked painedly at Reagan. "Is he in charge here, Lew?" He let his voice rise. "Am I to take his abuse?"

One of the men outside queried urgently, "Mr. Tillander? You in any trouble?"

Reagan whispered, "Tell 'em everything's fine and you want horses saddled up. Four fresh horses for a fast trip! Go on, tell 'em!"

Tillander searched Reagan's face narrowly. He nodded in thoughtful agreement to some calculation of his own, and, drawing a quick breath, he announced loudly, "I'm held up! Reagan and Carmack!"

Reagan swung his gun to slash him down, but halted the blow midway. The harm was done, and hitting Tillander could not repair it. And Tillander, observing that his close calculation was correct, finished his announcement:

"They're heavily armed, so watch out! Heckels is handcuffed. The girl's here with them, and you can tell everybody she's as tough as they are! Reagan figures to lead them in a breakout!"

He smiled at Reagan, while the men yelled the alarm for all the town to hear. "That's another bad thing about a hostage, Lew," he remarked in his normal tone. "No matter what he does, you can't kill him. You can threaten all you like, but if he has any brains he knows you're bluffing— because if you kill him he's no longer any use to you! Simple, isn't it? I think you'd better give up!"

"Why?"

"What chance have you got? You're bottled up! You've killed a couple of men, choked a woman, stuck up our deputy sheriff, and—well, it adds up to quite a list, for a stranger! Every man in town and for miles around is against you. They can shoot this place to pieces! Or burn you out!"

"Not the ranch folks," interposed Heckels. He spoke calmly. "I don't vouch for the town scum, but the ranch folks won't do any shooting or burning while a woman's in here. I mean Miss Harby."

Reagan unlocked the handcuffs from the deputy's wrists, and took them to Tillander. "And your scum won't shoot while you're with us, Frank, will they? Put your hands behind your back and turn around!" He fitted the handcuffs on Tillander and shoved him over to the window. "Now you just tell 'em to be careful!"

He turned to Heckels. "D'you believe she's Susan Harby? She is, you know."

"She's got proof," Jim Carmack put in, and Frank Tillander twisted to stare sharply at him. "Her father's papers, Amiel Harby's will, letters—in Colorado! A lawyer in her home town has them."

Rubbing his wrists gently, Heckels murmured, "First time

71

I ever knew what those things felt like. What? I guess I do."
He peered beneath bushed brows at Susan. "You ain't tough,
young lady. You look gamesome, but you're just a green
little pilgrim full of—uh—full of what makes a filly kick up
its heels. I've got a daughter not many years older'n you.
Can't tell you how relieved I was when she got safely
married to a good steady cowman. Was afraid she'd pick up
with some fly-by-night hot-shot!"

Reagan, the shift of topic not wholly to his liking, eyed
him coldly. Garrulous old gaffer, running off about his own
family affairs as if nothing else were important. He said to
him, "Heckels, you can go if you want to."

"I can walk out?" Heckels did not act surprised. "That's
handsome of you. I 'preciate it. My daughter—"

"Yeah. Wish you'd talk to your friends among the cattle
crowd. Tell 'em the same as you've said here, about Susan.
Maybe you can get 'em to lend a hand."

"On your side? Against Frank? Man, don't you ever let
go?"

"I've let go too often. Not this time!"

Heckels nodded understandingly. "Fly-by-night hot-shot,
hungry for—what? A wife and a roof, or just a certain
woman? Your kind is the saddest there is. No peace! Get
what you thought you wanted, and off you go again searching for something else. You die lonely."

"I'm not dead yet. Will you talk to the cattle crowd?"

They talked low-voiced for Frank Tillander not to hear.
"Oh, I'll do it," Heckels said. "I'll do it. But don't expect
anything. They got no outright quarrel with Frank. He's in
cattle, like them. They know you're a fly-by night, a dodger
—Longrider Reagan, Frank's called you, and he says you're
wanted in Texas for cattle rustling. Why would they side
you against him?"

"Susan?"

"I can't prove she ain't what Frank says she is, can I? A
fancy woman, using a false name. Comes into the country,
unmarried, camping in a wagon with a horse thief and a
gun-slinging . . . Don't glare at me, it ain't my opinion!"

A voice out front asked, "Where are you, Mr. Tillander?"

"By the window," Tillander answered.

"Stay clear of the door!" Shots roared close at hand and
the door shook, splintered in a dozen places.

Heckels shouted, "Hold off, I'm coming out! Me—
Heckels! Coming out!" The gunfire ceased and he moved
to the door.

"You'll try?" Reagan said to him.

"Sure, but what's the use?" Heckels paused to speak back and repeated. "What's the use? Frank's right. Give up, Reagan! Give them two a chance..." He gestured toward Susan and Jim.

"What kind of chance?"

"The chance to stay alive, which you haven't got in any case! I'd do my best for 'em. I'm deputy sheriff"—he drew his shoulders up—"and there are men still left who'd help stand guard if—"

"If! That's not good enough for me!"

"Not for you, no," Heckels granted. A bullet had punched the bolt on the door. He worked the mangled bolt loose, sighing. "I guess any man's afraid to die, Reagan. I just thought maybe you—"

"Let it go," said Reagan.

The emergence of Heckels from his office brought forth a barrage of questions, to which he evidently gave short reply, for presently the hubbub died and a fresh burst of shots struck the door and swept on through.

"D'you reckon he'll do us any good?" Jim Carmack asked.

Reagan's shrug was skeptical. "Maybe he won't try! Maybe these jiggers won't let him! But it was worth letting him go. He wasn't doing us any good here."

They and Susan kept to the wall on the window side of the office, out of the line of fire. Frank Tillander turned his back to the blanket-draped window, facing them, smiling. Even with his hands manacled behind him he maintained an air of self-assurance, of viewing the whole thing as a passing episode that only lightly affected him personally. Reagan was reminded that in the old days along the Texas border, with Harby and the others, Frank occasionally had exhibited that same cool detachedness in tight spots—always when he saw a way out for himself.

Susan had heard Heckels' words to Reagan. She moved up close and asked earnestly, "You won't give yourself up to them, Lew, will you?"

He raised his gaze from her face and met Jim's eyes. "Not likely!"

"I believe they'd kill you!"

"I wouldn't stand trial, that's sure! Would it hurt you?"

"Yes, Lew; as much as the death of a brother, if I had one."

"Um." It was a sincere compliment, Reagan supposed, though not what he had in mind. "Thanks!"

73

Frank Tillander, overhearing, murmured, "My jiggers don't believe in trials." His mocking smile grew more pronounced. "I'll miss you, *Brother!*"

He fell suddenly forward. As he fell, the blanket came dragging down off the window with him. Reagan grabbed at him too late, sank with him to the floor, and barked to Susan, "Down!" Frank Tillander's fall was a trick. He had clasped a fold of the blanket in his fingers, unseen behind him, and uncovered the window to pose the interior of the lighted office to the shooters outside.

"Now!" Tillander shouted. "Hit 'em now!"

Jim Carmack lunged at the lamp. Promptly a bullet punched a starred hole through the window. It passed between him and the lamp and dug a groove in the wall. He blew a tremendous puff over the lamp chimney, but the angle was wrong; the flame guttered smokily and rose again. The next bullet whipped a neat red slash across his throat. He picked up the lamp, hurled it at the window, and dropped to the floor.

The lamp crashed through the window and sailed on. It missed the blue wagon out front and smashed in the street, where it burst like a fire bomb. Some of Tillander's men, using the wagon as their cover, got confused and came tumbling out; and Reagan, lifting his head above the window sill, slammed three shots among them before he had to duck.

In one way the positions were now reversed: the office was dark and there was light outside. Reagan crawled back and got a rifle. He bumped into Jim and inquired, "You hit bad?"

"No, but it sure came close to the gullet! I'd like to ram that lamp down Tillander's throat!"

Frank Tillander laughed softly on the floor. "I told you, Lew! A hostage is a liability! I'll trip you any way I can, and you cant' stop me!"

"It was a nice try for a handcuffed man," Reagan allowed. "Guess I'll have to knock you out."

"Not smart, Lew! If they shout to me, and I don't answer, they'll think you've killed me! Then what?"

"Then they'll burn us out. And we'll leave you behind!"

Tillander clucked his tongue. "Tough on an old sidekick! I don't think you'd do it."

"We never were close friends—remember? Said so yourself, to Felisa Plevin. By the way, what's this about me

74

choking her? I didn't lay a hand on the woman. Should've! She tried to shoot Susan later with her little pocket gun."

"Yes? She's a jealous wildcat. I nearly strangled her dead," Tillander said matter-of-factly, "when I found she'd let Susan get away. What the hell, you've got to keep a woman in her place or she'll walk all over you!"

"I guess you're right."

"You know I am!"

"You two," observed Jim in the dark, "sound pretty cozy for a couple of hot-shots who aren't friends!"

"Oh, Lew and I understand each other," Tillander said. "We've seen the elephant and heard the owl hoot many a night." The gunfire recommenced on the door, and he called out, "You'll have to rush 'em! Reagan's loaded for war and he won't quit till you kill him!"

"Okay," a voice responded. "Give us time!"

A different voice, one with the powerful resonance of a bull, bellowed up the street, "Is that young woman in the jail? If she is, lay off the shootin' before she gets hurt! We don't fight women here!"

Tillander's man retorted that any woman who threw in with outlaws had only herself to blame if she got hurt, and an argument ensued, the bull-voiced man insisting that the shooting should cease.

"Somebody's on our side," Jim said hopefully. "The cattle crowd?"

"That's no crowd," Tillander drawled. "It's Eph Magee, with probably three or four of his old mossback cronies. They sit moaning about the good old days and damning everything new. Couldn't rope a dead calf—but talk? How they can talk!"

Soaring into a flight of loquacity, Eph Magee declared that no true man ever treated women with anything but profound respect; at least they didn't when he was young. Woman was heaven's gift to man, to be treasured as a jewel.

"Listen to the old buzzard!" Tillander said. "He's worn out three wives and worked his daughters like slaves, but he talks like a knight in shining armor!"

The mob jeered, their spokesman saying, "We'd set fire to the goddam place an' cut 'em down as they come out, if they wasn't holding Frank Tillander in there!"

The old man, vanquished, quit after bawling futilely something about women being like rare angels in the regard of true men of the old Western stock. The firing, which had slackened during the brief argument, was resumed, and

75

sounds announced that Tillander's men were not only surrounding the building but were on the flat roof as well. In thinking of the roof, and estimating its thickness, Reagan wondered if the men on it were digging down through it into the jail at the rear. He slid back over the floor of the office to investigate, meantime emptying his rifle at the front door to discourage a rush. Between his firing and the fusillade of the besiegers the door was disintegrating.

He paused, another idea occurring to him. "Look," he said, reloading the rifle. "Susan! You and I could walk out with Tillander. They wouldn't shoot. There are horses in the livery. We'd clear town and head for Ute!"

"Ute is a long ride," Jim Carmack objected. "You'd have to dodge and hide all the way, lifting fresh horses where you could! Six days would be making good time."

"What's time got to do with it?" Reagan demanded.

Jim didn't say. What he said was, "If anybody's taking Susan on that kind of trip, I'll do it!"

"You chesty tramp!" Reagan spoke bitingly. "You interfering nobody, you'd be bait for buzzards if it wasn't for me! Susan—"

The broken window became momentarily darkened. Frank Tillander, diving out through it, shouted, "Hold your fire—it's me!" His body banged on the boardwalk and they heard the sharp rap of his handcuffs as he rolled himself over and over off to the side. A cheer rose from his men.

The flames of the smashed lamp in the street burned blue, expiring. "And now," said Jim, "there's nothing left to stop 'em! Reagan, did you let him go on purpose, like you did Heckels?"

"You were nearer to him than I was!"

"Yeah—but you were friendlier!" Mutual animosity bred distrust and unreasoned accusations between them, and Jim worsened it with the searing comment "Nothing a longrider does would surprise me!"

"Shut your yap and watch the door!" Reagan snarled at him. "I'm giving a look at the rear."

"You haven't made a private deal with Tillander?"

"Like what?"

"Like, maybe, he gives you a getaway with Susan, if you'll—"

"I've got a mind to crack your skull for that, Carmack!"

"Okay. Sorry. But you've been riding me rough from the start!"

"Let it go."

"And you've made plain your feelings and what you'd do about—"

"Let it go, I said!"

Ten

ALTHOUGH, AS JIM had said, there was nothing left to stop the mob from setting fire to the jail building after Frank Tillander dived out the window, a nerve-racking hour of comparative quiet dragged by. The men on the roof stopped moving about, and those in the street kept up only a desultory sniping at the door and window.

The delay was guaranteed to stretch the nerves cruelly, and for a while Reagan thought that might be its purpose. Speculating further, he figured it more probable that the intervention of loudmouthed Eph Magee and his cronies remained a deterrent. Tillander was unwilling to bring down upon himself the condemnation of the cattle crowd. He would exhaust all other means first.

It would have to be a rush. To look out the door or window was suicide, with the snipers alertly covering them at short range, but on the other hand the snipers weren't free to show themselves either. Reagan listened intently, measuring sounds for signs of a rush in the making. He and Jim Carmack checked and loaded all firearms in the deputy's office, and, having laid them out ready, they could only wait.

The signs began building up, an accumulation of telltale sounds, at first tentative, becoming definite. Men on the roof renewed their movements. There were low mutterings around the building, and something solid scraped the side wall. Running on tiptoe across the street to the wagon, somebody stumbled and swore softly. The intermittent sniping ceased.

The silence, overlaid on a rustle of hushed activity, gave the final cue. "Here they come!" Reagan said.

They closed in, maintaining their silence until Jim, timing their advance to the last instant, cut loose a rapid-fire blast at the door with a rifle. It was as if he fired into a case of shells and set them off. The remains of the door collapsed before the guns of the attackers, and the window became a shot-lit square. A man burst through the doorway, shouting furiously while pitching forward onto his face. Another tripped on him, threw his arms wide for balance, and, meeting a bullet, he fell back and blocked the rush. Reagan left the doorway to Jim Carmack and concentrated on the win-

78

dow. Above the din he heard then the blows of an ax chopping a hole in the roof at the rear.

Jim slid his emptied rifle to Susan for reloading and grabbed another, but Susan snatched up the deputy's shotgun instead and fled through the rear door. Somebody shoved the wounded man aside and dragged the fallen one out by his heels, loosening the jam. The window cleared for a moment, and Reagan dropped his rifle and flipped out his guns. He blazed at the doorway. A tangle of men again choked it. He was counting his shots, not sure whether a loaded rifle was left or if Jim Carmack was using it up, when the shotgun blared in the jail.

A man on the roof raised a high wail, and the shotgun exploded its second load. The ax clattered along the roof, thrown in rage. Somebody up there yelled, "God damn it, she got me! Look at my foot!"

Considering the number of hardcases that Frank Tillander was able to enlist on brief notice, Reagan expected the onslaught to continue regardless of injuries. Its first failure was not to be taken as conclusive, but as temporary at most, providing him and Jim Carmack the chance to reload and prepare for the next rush.

The tangle at the door dissolved. The window stayed clear. Sounds on the roof told of an injured man being helped down off it. Susan came in from the jail for fresh shells for the shotgun and left the connecting door open. In a little while the sniping was resumed from points across the dark street, but nobody took up station again behind the blue wagon.

"They've only pulled back for a better go at it," Reagan warned Jim. He heard Jim murmuring to Susan, and he said harshly, "Don't let down!"

As time passed, though, he let himself gradually relax. The smoke of burned powder had irritated his eyelids so that they felt granulated, and the smell of it was an acrid residue in his nostrils, the taste metallic in his dry throat. He massaged his eyes gently with his knuckles, blew his nose, hawked and spat. The tricks for easing strained nerves entailed a technique that was private and altogether his own.

One trick that he had developed was to bring to his mind, by an effort of will, the day he reluctantly took a neighbor girl fishing and returned full of strange glory and a marriage vow, at the age of thirteen. In visualizing that day in every particular, the past took on kindly humor, and the present, however pressing, receded into a more adaptable perspective.

If for any reason that didn't work, he had always been able to fall back on a form of fatalism, a stark philosophy that held for him the principle that probably what was to be would be and if not to hell with it because nothing mattered very much. That, too, put the present in its place.

Now the neighbor girl and the long-gone day eluded him. And everything mattered.

Scrabbling for the reason why Tillander's hardcases were holding back, it occurred to him that he had not heard Tillander's voice among them. Had not, in fact, heard anything of Tillander since he dived out through the window.

"Did you happen to hear Frank out there?" he asked Jim. And Jim said, no, he hadn't, come to think of it. "Maybe he got damaged," Reagan said. "Something's keeping 'em waiting. They'd be at us again before now, if he was there to crack the whip."

"Perhaps," Susan ventured hopefully, "he's had a change of heart."

"Tillander?" Jim said. "Not that snaky-eyed devil!"

"Never had a heart to begin with," said Reagan.

They lay on guard through the few remaining hours of darkness. For three nights Reagan had gone without sleep except for brief naps, mostly in the saddle. It was a practice gained from longrider necessity, but the drain was telling on him. His eyes were too dry and heavy to function correctly, and refused to hold focus for any length of time. More and more often everything swam in a blur and his mind went blank. He sank his head onto his forearm on the floor. Closing his eyes gave him vast relief. Jim Carmack was wide awake and on the *cuidado,* he assured himself, Not because Carmack was younger. No. Nothing to do with it. Carmack had been able to get some sleep in jail, all any man needed to last him . . .

"Reagan?"

"Um? Whassup?" he mumbled.

Jim had crawled over to him. "I guess you fell asleep."

"Me? Hell, no!" He had taken the neighbor girl fishing. He had relived that sunny day to the moment when, incredibly, he was glad he'd taken her along. "Didn't sleep a wink!"

"It's getting light."

"Sure it is." He sat up cautiously, paying a bleary-eyed look to the door and window. "What did you do for coffee and grub in the jail?"

80

"It was brought from the cafè, but I don't see 'em doing it this morning," Jim said. "Susan's fast asleep."

"I'm awake now," Susan spoke up, and they watched her come out on hands and knees from behind the pile of Harby belongings. She appeared refreshed, though tousled. It struck Reagan that she looked quite a bit like that neighbor girl. Copper hair all streaming, face glowing. Her figure, of course, had a more ripened quality, more highly provocative... Even on this dismal morning the effect was ravishing, if not downright wanton.

They had finished the deputy's bottle of water, so Reagan made do with some of the whiskey that was left. Susan declined his offer of the same, saying that she wasn't that thirsty, and Jim didn't seem to relish whiskey for breakfast. Reagan drank the rest of it, feeling slightly sordid, like a dissolute prodigal in church. He sent the empty bottle rolling out the door. Somebody blew it to bits with a bullet. Probably a puritan, he thought sourly; some bigoted buzzard who abhorred early drinking, if there was any such freak in Cochimi.

The bullet marked the end of the night seige, for a band of horsemen clattered into town with the sunrise and caused distraction along the street. Chancing a quick look out the window and seeing Deputy Sheriff Heckels at their head, Reagan welcomed for once the arrival of a law officer. "Maybe we'll get a meal now," he told Susan and Jim. His eating had been sketchy the last couple of days. "It's our dauntless deputy with some of the cattle crowd."

Much time elapsed, taken up with arguments interrupted by jeering catcalls, before Heckels stepped up onto the boardwalk, calling, "Drop the shooting, in there!"

"Who's shooting?" Reagan retorted.

Heckels came in, stepping over the wreckage of the door. He scanned sorrowfully his bullet-scarred office. "My Lord!" he complained. "Who'll pay the bill to fix this up?" He gazed at Reagan, then at Susan and Jim. "You look like hell, the three of you!"

"Took you long enough to get back!" Reagan said. "How about breakfast?"

Heckels gazed at Reagan a moment longer and said with rising wrath, "I been out riding all night for you, and that's the thanks I get! It's summer. Cowmen are all busy. Some of 'em have took time off to come in with me. Don't it mean anything to you?"

"It means they're doing what they ought to do! This is their town! They'll help you clean it up!"

"Wrong!" Heckels snapped. "They won't do your fighting for you, Reagan! Their only concern is the young woman. She ought to be let out of it before she gets hurt. They support me on that. But they can't stay long. Too busy."

"Is that as far as they'll go?"

"That's it!"

Reagan shook his head. "They're not supporting you, Heckels! Why?"

"I've told you. It's summer, and they're too busy—"

"No! It's because they've seen you knuckling under to Tillander and they just don't look up to you any more. They're licked, like you! Licked without a fight!"

Heckels bawled, "Who, me? Now see here—"

"They've ridden in with you to ask Tillander politely if he'll kindly do 'em a favor to stop the shooting for a spell! It'd look bad if they let Susan get killed!" Reagan's voice grew grating. "They're high-minded cattle folks, all swelled up with respect for women! Got to live up to it! After they nobly save her life, of course, what becomes of her is none of their business. Too busy! Their goddam cows are more important!"

Heckels swallowed, taken aback by the blast. "You don't understand. They still think she's just a—a—"

"Fancy woman?" Reagan said bluntly. "What the hell's the difference what a woman is, if she needs help? Why, damn their peanut souls, I've known a Lulu or two who . . ." He checked himself, aware that Susan was listening. "Bring your friends in here and let me talk to 'em!"

"Wouldn't do much good," Heckels demurred, with a doubtful glance at Susan. "Take more'n talk to change their minds. And I'd have to ask Frank in on it, too, or he'd think I was working against him." A meager grin crossed his bearded face. "Frank ain't got the handcuffs off yet. They're hand forged and hardened. The smithy's on a drunk and everybody's been taking a crack at 'em. You've got my keys."

It explained why Frank Tillander had not taken an active part in the seige, and why the jail building had not been set on fire. Reagan nodded. "Bring him in with the others. But no monkeyshines!"

He turned to Susan when Heckels had left. "All right, let's get to work on you!" She and Jim sent him blank stares, and he said impatiently, "If they're so lily-white pure, we've got to play up to 'em! They judge a woman by her appearance, and yours... Well, for one thing, your hair... Tie it back for her, Carmack! Kind of tight. Y'know, like an onion."

They brushed and straightened her dress, seated her in the deputy's chair so that her bare feet didn't show, and tied her hair straight back in a severe knot. They hadn't much time, and their experience for the task was limited. And Susan was not altogether co-operative, she having some positive ideas of her own about how to wear clothes and fix her hair. But they succeeded in effecting something of a transformation that, although not an artistic improvement, at least subdued some of her natural vividness.

"Pity we can't tone down, er—un!" Reagan coughed. "I guess we've done all we can!"

When Heckels and Tillander and half-a-dozen cattlemen trooped in, Susan was sitting with her hands folded primly in her lap, hair skinned back and feet tucked out of sight. She was a decorous young schoolma'am, dedicated to plain duty and no nonsense. The cattlemen eyed her approvingly.

"Gentlemen," said Reagan, "this is Miss Harby, as I think you know. Amiel Harby was her uncle. Her father—"

"She's an impostor!" Frank Tillander broke in. Compared to his former assurance, he appeared considerably ruffled. The hours in handcuffs had turned his mood savage. His wrists were burned and bruised from inept attempts to free them. "She's just a..." Seeing the stern looks directed at him by the cattlemen, he paused, then said more moderately, "It's hard to believe!"

Eph Magee had attached himself importantly to the group. "In this country," he declared, "we don't question the word of a good woman! We don't call her names! In the good old days we'da hanged any blagyard who did!" He wore a white goatee and had the intolerant eyes of an old-timer disdainful of the current crop of upstarts.

Tillander inclined his head. "And rightly so, Mr. Magee! It was your splendid generation, sir, that brought culture and chivalry to this wild country, and I honor it! Nor do I stand second to any man," he went on suavely, "in my honor and respect for American womanhood!"

Flattered and mollified, old Eph Magee queried, "Well, fine, but didn't you question the young lady's word?"

"No!" Tillander disclaimed. "I question the word of Longrider Reagan. I suspect the motives of any man with his record! And I can't help wondering at—ah—Miss Harby's

83

connection with him! Not to mention the horse thief, Carmack!"

The eyes of the cattlemen turned back on Susan

"Carmack resisted arrest, and she tried to help him," Tillander pressed on. "She escaped from my custody, with Reagan's help! They held up Heckels, broke Carmack out of his cell, and the three of them have stood the town off all night! Strange company for a young lady!"

"They're my friends!" Susan protested. Then she became confused under the battery of inquiring eyes. "They helped me," she said faintly, and the faces of the cattlemen lost their kindly approval. "I—I don't know what I'd do without Lew and Jim!" she insisted.

There was silence. Frank Tillander ended it by blandly inquiring, "This is Miss Harby, a young schoolma'am? This is the virtuous young lady who claims to inherit Amiel Harby's property? Hah! An outlaw's angel! A lying little impostor!"

Nobody objected to his language this time, not even old Eph Magee. The group only shifted uncomfortably, gazing anywhere but at Susan.

Eleven

REAGAN SIGHED. They were ready to abandon her, let her go to the devil—because of the company she was in, because of her innocent admission of dependence on a couple of dodgers. Frank Tillander had smartly blackened her case before this impromptu jury of stiff-necked mossbacks in whose severe judgment only two kinds of women existed, the good and the fallen, with a gulf yawning between them as wide as the gap between heaven and hell.

"I'll tell you how I came to help her," Reagan said slowly. He had to choose his words with care and not say too much. "Her father, Allen Harby, was killed coming down here from Colorado. Shanty Green and two others fired on the wagon. I killed one of 'em and put his horse with the team. It was a Rocking H nag!"

"A neat story," Tillander commented. "The part I can believe is where you killed a man for his horse! What happened to Shanty Green?"

"You know! He tried to ambush me on the Piedras Gordas. He had Allen Harby's rifle. I dropped him and came back to find out why you sent him to get me!"

"That's two men he admits killing, gentlemen! He's trying to claim self-defense. Trying to claim I had something to do with it. Hogwash!" Tillander smiled around at the cattlemen. Their faces registered thoughtful doubt, but he retained his smile. "Hogwash!" he repeated. "He's a killer! Last night he took over this jail at gun point. He refused to give up, and shot several of our local citizens who—"

"Wait a minute!" Jim Carmack cut in. "You can't hang it all on him! We were in it together, fighting off that mob out there!"

"You bragging?" Reagan snapped. "It was me did all the shooting!"

"What?" Jim blinked at him. "Man, I—"

"Shut up!"

Deputy Sheriff Heckels gazed from one to the other and wagged his head. "Are you clearing Carmack of any part in all this?" he asked Reagan. "Why?"

Reagan could have told him why, but not easily, although

the answer was plain to him. Because Susan will need somebody to look after her. *And it can't be me!* Can't hang on here, can't shoot my way out, and I'm in too deep to care how many charges they add to the list. Let it go. Nothing matters.

He said, "I picked up Carmack in the Gila badlands, afoot and out of water. Afterwards, he drove the Harby wagon. Just a hired man, working for his grub. Took his orders from me!"

Jim opened his mouth to speak, but Heckels said, "That clears him in my book. Nor I don't see cause any more to hold the young lady, unless somebody's got a complaint and wants to swear out a warrant. You, Mr. Tillander?"

"Why me?" Tillander's look was poisonous. "Ask the man whose toes she shotgunned off last night on the roof! As for me, what I've said about her still stands. An outlaw's angel! You can't believe her kind! Barefaced liars and cheats, every one!"

"Now, Mr. Tillander—"

"What's her connection with this killer? He says he's only been helping her. Hah! What was the game they cooked up together? I'll tell you! It was to lay claim to the Rocking H, my ranch! I ask you, gentlemen, would a man like this Longrider Reagan—this killer—lend his help for nothing? Why? Out of the goodness of his heart?"

"It's a fair question," admitted Eph Magee, and the others nodded. "He's sure gone a far piece of his way for her! Course, any of *us* would," he hastened to add, "for a good woman who needs help. But him? For a *good* woman? Why?"

Heckels cocked an expressionless eye at Reagan. "Why?" he echoed.

There it was again, the suspicion, based on the prejudiced proverb that birds of a feather flocked together. The belief, Christian teachings to the contrary, that a man could be judged from his company; likewise a woman. The cruelly blind tradition that a woman, losing her good name, must be shunned as bad all through. Reagan sighed once more, wearily angry. His anger was not aimed at Frank Tillander, but at these people, typical of their kind anywhere they lived their narrow and insular lives; these self-righteous people; these proud prigs. Tillander was merely trading on their prejudices, and from the broadest viewpoint Reagan could hardly blame him for doing it.

He walked to the window and stared out, letting them

wait for his reply to that critical question: *Why?* Much as he disliked the nickname that had been fastened onto him back in Texas years ago, he felt like a worn and frowzy longrider, a man without much aim in life, addicted to transient gains and pagan pleasures.

He turned to them abruptly and said, "When I saw her father I thought he was Amiel Harby. Looked just like him. I knew Amiel Harby some years ago in Texas. Knew him well."

Heckels lifted an eyebrow. "So?"

"He owed me money. I figured to collect it. He was dead, but he'd left property. Left it to his brother, her father. Well, there her father was dead, too, leaving her to inherit—"

"I get it!" old Eph Magee crowed triumphantly. "We was right, Mr. Tillander! He wasn't helping her for nothing! He had a stake in it!"

"Sure," Reagan said. "I had to look after my interests. Aimed to clinch a hold on her, maybe even marry her for the property if I had to!"

"Trust your kind to watch out for Number One!"

"That's me." Reagan avoided looking at Susan. "It didn't work, though. Come to find out, Tillander holds the Rocking H. And I couldn't make any time with *her*." He pushed through them to the inner door of the jail. "Damn it, I tried, but she's not my kind! Not by a long shot, she isn't! All right, Heckels . . ."

Heckels followed him into the jail. "Your guns, Reagan," he requested temperately. "And I'll have my keys back now." He closed and locked the cell door, and stood for a moment gazing through the bars at his prisoner "Didn't think you'd ever give up, after you turned me down last night. See things different this morning, eh?"

Reagan took a seat on the hard bunk. He forced a gaunt grin. "I was getting hungry," he said. "How about breakfast?"

Bringing him his breakfast from the café, Heckels volunteered to Reagan the information that he was booked on a variety of charges including murder.

"The circuit judge is due through here next month. He'll hear your case. Just a formality. You'll be bound over for trial and taken—"

"I'm not looking forward to the long and dreary processes of law," Reagan said, eating. "Only two eggs?"

"It's all the budget allows. No, I don't look forward to it

either. A lot can happen in a month." Heckels paused. "Eph Magee and the others are escorting Miss Harby out to my son-in-law's place. My daughter'll be glad of her company. Carmack's gone along too. My son-in-law needs a rider. Miss Harby can stay there while we check with that Colorado lawyer. I don't much doubt the outcome. Tillander will sure fight her claim to the Rocking H, though!"

"But not in court! If he holds a bill of sale, it's a forgery. I'll lay any bet that the title deed is still in Amiel Harby's name." Reagan ate in silence for a while, thinking of Susan and Jim. "You're right, a lot can happen in a month. Frank Tillander won't be idle!"

"He wants a talk with you. In private, he says. He's waiting outside now."

"I'm not surprised. Let him stew while I catch some sleep. You can bring him in when I wake up."

"Yes, sir," said Heckels dryly, taking the empty plate. "Anything to please a guest in this hotel."

Yawning, Reagan stretched out on the bunk and turned his face to the wall. In a minute he was fast asleep.

Heckels didn't show Frank Tillander into the jail until midafternoon. Reagan, awake, was lying on the bunk, reviewing his situation and mentally casting up the odds against its betterment. He sat up as the two men came to his cell door. "Visitor to see you," Heckels announced, reverting somewhat self-consciously to his dry pretense of servility.

Frank Tillander, however, chose to take the pretense for actuality and said to him, "Thanks, you can leave us now. I want to see Reagan alone." He outstared the deputy sheriff, who, having already strained their ambiguous relationship to the breaking point, decided to capitulate this time and walked back to his office.

Waiting until the connecting door was closed, Tillander said quietly to Reagan, "You held out something this morning when you made your talk to Heckels and the cowmen."

Reagan stretched his arms and back and groaned comfortably. "Um! About you tracking Harby down here, on an old grudge. About you being the one with plenty of motive for killing him. And a couple more little facts about you."

"That's right. Why?"

"You have to ask?"

They eyed each other impassively through the bars. Then Tillander smiled. He offered Reagan a cigar. "I've got to hand it to you, Lew! Never knew you to be without a card of

88

some kind up your sleeve. That's your last card, though, eh?"

"Just about." Reagan bit off the end of the cigar and took a light from Tillander's match.

"And you'll play it for all it's worth! Okay. What d'you want? Out?"

"What else d'you offer?"

"Nothing!" Tillander said. "And there's a string to it. If I get you out, you quit this country. Mexico's not bad. You keep your mouth shut and don't ever come back here!"

"And leave this field all to you, um?"

"Sure. Can you stop me? Nobody can! Our mutual friend, the little lady—"

"Susan Harby," Reagan pronounced carefully.

Tillander shrugged. "Susan Harby, yes. You and I both know she can prove claim to the Rocking H, given a little time. Am I the kind of fool that would let her have the time? Are *you*? I took trouble and risk to get hold of that outfit. To keep it, I'd make her marry me if I had to! Not an unpleasant chore, that!"

"You'd have the whole country down on you. Heckels' son-in-law—"

"Bill Gillespie? His is a two-bit spread, no crew. Just himself and a younger brother, and now Carmack. And a few friends hanging around for the time being." Tillander laughed softly. "How long will they stay alert? They're not like us, Lew, these good folks—they'll soon slack off!"

"And then?" Reagan asked.

"Then," Tillander said elegantly, "the unguarded blossom may be plucked, quickly, while their attention wanders! No trouble with them, and no complaining from her afterwards —not publicly, at least!"

"You think not, Frank?"

"Her, you mean? You don't know women like I do, Lew!"

They both were silent, each occupied with differing musings, until Reagan, glanced up, found Tillander's light blue eyes fixed strangely upon him. Tillander looked swiftly away, and said, "Around midnight you'll hear shots somewhere on the edge of town. That's the signal. We'll raise a riot. While it's going on, we'll wrench the bars from your window with the smithy's chain pulley. There'll be a fast horse ready for you."

"And a gun?"

Tillander's hesitation lasted only an instant. "Sure!"

Sure, Reagan thought, an empty gun. You wouldn't give a

89

loaded gun to a man you intend killing. Riot and jail break. Run, prisoner, run—but not far. Shots. Killed by citizens while attempting desperate escape with the help of unknown accomplices. A lawful deed, no discredit to anyone. Hooray for the *ley del fuego,* the efficient Mexican method of eliminating an awkward prisoner.

"That's your top offer, Frank? Horse, gun and a getaway?" He was playing for time to probe it for possible loopholes, while holding to the pretense of straightforward bargaining.

"I'm being generous, Lew! For old times' sake."

"Let's not get all choked up."

Tillander flattened out a hand in a gesture of finality. "Let's not," he murmured. "I *could* arrange a lynching bee!"

Could, Reagan thought; yes, using the Hi Jolly mob. And you will, if I turn down your offer. You can't afford to let me live and go on trial. What I know about you would explode the court. You can't afford to wait, either, while Heckels gets in touch with the Colorado lawyer. You must' act fast, and you will, one way or other. Susan has only a thin and temporary protection, Jim Carmack is a Jonah who'll break his neck dashing to help her, and I'm stuck in this stinkingly tight jail. Time is pushing all of us.

His one last card shrank dismally in value. He couldn't detect the slightest loophole in Tillander's simple trap. Perhaps he would be able to make one somehow when the time came. It was a forlorn gamble, a fraction better than the dead certainty of a lynching bee.

"About midnight, um?"

"Right. S'long till then, Lew."

"S'long, Frank . . ."

Twelve

DEPUTY SHERIFF HECKELS came back into the jail after Til-
lander left. He brought with him an early-evening meal for
Reagan. For some time, in preoccupied fashion, he watched
Reagan eating. Finally he spoke.

"Maybe I ought to tell you I'm staying on watch all night
from now on! I ain't fixed the busted door and window yet
in my office, nor that hold up there in the roof, but I'll have
a loaded shotgun, two rifles, and four six-guns handy! Just
in case!"

Reagan swallowed a morsel of beef and washed it down
with coffee. "In case what?"

"Well, in case ... For one thing, Bill Gillespie, my son-
in-law, has sent me word that some of the young cowpokes
are rattlin' their spurs round Susan Harby. His young
brother, Chris, is one of 'em. Romantic, y'know. They're
panting to help her. If she asked 'em to bring her the man
in the moon, they'd take a crack at it. Never can tell what
fit might take a bunch of wild younkers like them. 'Specially
with a pretty girl to play up to. She's dangerous!"

"So's a kitten. You don't know her." Reagan shook his
head. "She can't shoot worth a—"

"It could be real damn' bad," Heckels pursued, "if they
tangled with these town hooligans or the Rocking H riders.
They'd get wiped out in a minute! Just kids, acting man-
size. I wish," he said slowly and distinctly, "—I wish to God
you had never come here! I'd give anything if you and that
young woman—and Carmack, too—had stayed clear out o'
the territory!"

"Too late." Reagan slid the dishes out beneath the cell
door. "You loaded up for cockerels?"

"No, I wouldn't need to. Known 'em since they were
born. My friends' sons." Heckels picked up the dishes, carefully noting that the knife and fork were included. "Devil
knows this town was bad enough. Now it's worse, and spreading down into the valley like a disease. You shook it out!
You and Susan Harby! No, I'm loaded for other game if it
shows up!"

"Such as ... ?" Reagan asked.

Heckels laid a long look on him. "I can only guess," he said, turning away. "One thing I do know. You don't get to use those younkers and lead 'em into crazy mischief! Your kind's too often the downfall of young cowpokes!"

"How would I do that?" Reagan called after him.

"Something's in the wind, like you breaking out, or getting broke out," Heckels rasped over his shoulder. "You try it, I swear I'll shoot you dead!" He walked on up front into his office and left the connecting door open.

There would be competition tonight, Reagan reflected, among those who were dedicated to killing him. Open season on Longrider Lew Reagan. The deputy sheriff, though smart in some ways, had a mental quirk that led him to jump to conclusions without examining them. He wasn't using his head if he thought that Frank Tillander was about to break his prisoner out of jail in order to let him go and rouse up those cockerel cowpokes who were hanging around Susan. There wasn't a chance of making contact with those cockerels. Tillander would see to that, a shot ahead of Heckels.

"Ten to one on Frank!" Reagan muttered.

Heckels worked in his office by lamplight after sundown, and didn't make his evening rounds of the town. Around ten o'clock he put out the lamp and lay down on the cot, but he didn't sleep; Reagen heard him get up every so often and go to the front door. The deputy was keeping sharp check, his anxious suspicions probably supported by his veteran lawman's instinct for sensing trouble brewing. He would do a lot better, Reagan mused, to rely more on his hunches rather than follow the dictates of his imperfect intelligence. Any gambling man knew that.

As midnight advanced, noise rose in a steadily increasing roar from down along the lower section of the main street. Reagan's cell window, heavily barred and without glass, faced onto the alley between the jail and Visaya's Saddle Shop. By pushing his face against the bars he could glimpse a small segment of the street. Its shadows were cast by light reflected from the Hi Jolly, and he guessed most of the noise came from there.

A gnarled old cottonwood grew within a few feet of his window, further blocking his view. And Señor Visaya had added a wing to the back of his shop, closing off the alley at its rear end. The fact that it was a blind alley gave Reagan no comfort. If he managed by some miracle to survive his supposed rescue, he would have to take to the main street, where he'd show up like a moose in a melon patch.

But if he didn't go out, if he remained here in the dark cell—which began to strike him now as not a bad place to be in—then Tillander would simply fall back on an alternative method. A lynching bee. Or spray the cell with buckshot. Or heave in a fused canister of blasting powder. Something definitely fatal.

"Either way, I'm a goner!"

He sat down on the bunk to wait. Riot and jail break. They would rig the smithy's chain pulley to the trunk of the cottonwood, hook onto the window bar frame and wrench it loose, and—*Fly out of your cage, birdie, we've got nice crumbs for you!* Yup; leaden crumbs for . . .

Shots cracked somewhere, four of them, unevenly spaced, each echoing sharply, evidently fired between buildings. A woman screamed, loud and long, a scream of anguish that brought Reagan to his feet and set his neck hairs prickling. One more shot, and the scream trailed off into a shuddering wail of dreadful pain, then expired.

For a moment dead silence gripped the town. That awful shriek had penetrated even the noise of the Hi Jolly, frozen its customers, and stilled the piano. The hush broke with a rush of trampling feet and startled shouts. Reagan heard Heckels lunge up off the cot and go charging out.

"Where was it?" Heckels bawled in the street. "Where's that woman? Where . . ." A score of voices shouted different opinions as he ran off searching for murder.

It did not occur to Reagan that the thing could have been faked. The scream was too chillingly genuine, and the time still lacked half an hour to midnight. He did not think of it as the signal until footsteps sounded muffledly overhead. He jumped to the cell door and stared up through its bars. Somebody was easing himself down through the chopped hole in the roof.

First the legs, then the body. The man lowered himself, hung by his hands, dropped, and landed lightly on his feet. Instead of a hat he wore a white rag around his head. He turned swiftly to the cell door.

"The keys, Reagan! Where does Heckels keep 'em?"

"Keys?" Reagan muttered, scowling at him. It was Jim Carmack, bandaged head and all. "What're you doing here. Where's Susan?"

"Waiting with the horses—or she will be when we get there. A bit south of town, under some cottonwoods right of the road."

"You brought her in? Why, you—"

"Try and stop her, when she found I was coming in! The keys, Reagan! Where?"

"Heckels keeps 'em in his pants pocket. And he's gone looking for a screaming corpse! I mean a murdered female."

"Damn!" Jim breathed. "How do we get you out?"

"Alive? That question's been bothering me." Reagan curbed an urge to swear at him. After all, Jim had risked coming in for him, and it wasn't his fault about the keys. But that bad luck of his was certainly persistent. "My guns are in Heckels' desk. Get 'em!"

Jim brought him his guns and belts and thrust them through the bars. "How did you get onto the roof without anybody seeing you?" Reagan asked him.

"Climbed the back of the saddle shop next door."

"Go back the same way, quiet and fast as you can. Friends are breaking me out any minute now. Tillander and company!"

"You trust him?"

"Not one damn bit!" Reagan buckled on his guns. "But he'll crack open this cage, which is more'n we can do! The lock on this door, a bullet wouldn't dent it."

"I'll wait for Heckels and stick him up for the keys," Jim said.

"You won't," Reagan contradicted. "I hear chains clinking. They're coming in a hurry! Get to Susan and the horses! A bit south of town, you said? Watch out for me there. If I don't make it, you both ki-yi back to Gillespie's place and lay low!"

"Your chances look slim to me." Jim demurred. "That alley—and you'll have to climb out the window . . ."

"All the chance in the world," Reagan lied. "Go on, beat it!"

He watched Jim spring upward, catch the edge of the hole with his fingers, and draw himself up through, out onto the roof. His guns, buckled under his coat, butts forward, felt right. He gave Jim silent thanks for them. Pretty square of Jim to come in for him. Then the thought rose: Hell, why shouldn't he? Didn't I pull him off the frying lid of hell up there in the Gila badlands? Besides, he and Susan need me, and he knows it.

The rattling of the chains grew louder. There wasn't much effort at caution on the part of the men handling them. They knew that the deputy sheriff was out of earshot. A good deal of commotion was being raised by groups of searchers running noisily to and fro, arguing in loud voices. It wasn't a riot, but the Hi Jolly mob was busily creating an imitation of one. Reagan stepped to the window and peered out. Four men worked briskly at anchoring the chain pulley to the cottonwood trunk. One of them carried the chain hook to the window. Reagan moved back. The man lapped the chain around the bars. He laid an object on the sill.

"Gun!" he murmured, and retreated.

Reagan took the gun and felt it in the darkness. An old Dragoon .44, converted to cartridge. He broke it open. It was fully loaded, which surprised him. He punched out the shells and fingered them. They were fresh shells, their center-fire caps undented. Fingering them further, he felt scars in the sides of the bullets, left by the jaws of pliers, and he understood. The bullets had been pulled, the powder emptied from the cartridge cases, and the bullets replaced. A primer cap would explode when struck, and possibly have enough force to push the bullet feebly out of the gun muzzle, but that was all. The shells were a grim joke. The gun was no more lethal than a child's popgun.

The chains clicked whirringly in the sheaves, gathering up the slack, and the hook tightened with a hard jolt, and the loose clicking changed to a series of short tugs as the men hauled at the pulley chain. Something had to give way under the terrific strain. The bars bowed a little, but they were welded to the frame and would not part. What yielded was the iron bolts holding the frame. They were imbedded into the wall and they tore free, grinding, bent like nails drawn with a claw hammer. The whole frame came loose, and hands grasped it hurriedly and lowered it to the ground.

"Okay, Reagan!" said the same voice. "Out!"

The opening was not large. Reagan looked out and saw the four men backing abreast to the mouth of the alley leaving tackle and bar frame lying where they had dropped them. Two more men joined the four, and in the street beyond them he glimpsed others standing as motionless as entranced spectators at the climactic moment of a bullfight, when the toreador's sword hovers over the doomed bull.

He would have to emerge head first, a helpless target. The question was: Would they give him the chance, that tiny chance to get clear of the window? He made his rapid calculations and reckoned that they probably would. This thing was staged as the legitimate killing of a dangerous escapee; they believed that he was armed only with a useless gun and therefore they had no reason for rushing the execution.

95

And even the most debased gunmen generally liked to cloak murder in the guise of justified homicide, to be able to claim that the victim faced them with a gun and had a fair shake.

Holding the Dragoon .44 in his fist, he hooked his arms over the sill and heaved himself up. As his head and the upper part of his body emerged, the men at the mouth of the alley became as motionless as the watchers behind them. They stood blackly silhouetted against the weak light of the street, their shadowed faces craned forward, waiting, and he realized that he was wholly in shadow and could be seen by them only in outline.

He scraped on through the window until, his torso outweighing his legs, he tossed the gun forward, spread his hands, and let himself topple out. His hands struck the ground, elbows bent to take the jar of his fall, and, curving his back, he rolled clear over and came to his feet in a single flow of movement. He kicked the loose chains of the pulley and his stumble carried him closer to the cottonwood trunk, where he stooped low in search of the Dragoon.

The lean click of a cocked hammer sounded among the faceless, silent figures. They wanted him to hear that warning click of betrayal, wanted to rattle him into popping off the useless pistol and to die with it in his hand—as a private joke and a public brag: *Got hold of a gun and shot it out with us, but we downed the big cuss!*

He stayed stooped, only lifting his head to watch them, the armed men committed to the task of killing him. The one who had spoken to him through the cell window, their leader, asked, "Can't you find it, for hell's sake?"

"I've got it," Reagan said, coming upright.

"Good!" the man drawled softly. "Why don't you try it out?" Then impatiently, "Try it out, you goddam son—"

"*You* try it!"

He threw it, a fast underhand throw. They saw the movement of his arm, saw the glint of the long barrel flipping end over end at them, and all instinctively ducked their heads to let it fly past. He made his double cross-draw, two quick slaps, while shifting, putting the cottonwood between himself and them. Their leaded exclaimed, "Watch out!" his voice pinched thin, his cocked gun spearing a flash that in the dark alley seemed eight feet long and enormously loud.

Reagan fired at him. The man folded both arms over his middle, turning away, shaking his head as if in protest of a shocking outrage. He shouldered into another man, who,

96

shoving him off, blazed a wild shot as Reagan fired again, and rocked back crying out, "He's got his guns! Holy—"

Counting his shots, Reagan worked both guns, weaving from one side to the other of the cottonwood. The watchers in the street scattered out of the line of fire. A third man of the squad suddenly turned tail and ran. The remaining three jumped for the near corners of the sheriff's office and the saddle shop, where some of those who had been watching joined them in firing blindly into the alley.

He was bottled up. With as much calmness as he could muster, he confronted the fact that he was done for, that he might as well not have regained his guns. Their possession afforded him the satisfaction of going out fighting, of reversing the sardonic joke back on his executioners, but the end result was the same: Run, prisoner, run—but not far. *Ley del fuego* . . .

A rifle cracked off a shot, then three more in rapid series, giving notice that it was a repeater. The reports cut high-pitched through the heavier and nearer discharge of hand-guns, and brought a pause to the firing as though a voice of authority imposed order upon chaos. Reagan wondered detachedly how the rifleman proposed to snipe his mark here in the alley unless he had climbed to an overlooking place of vantage somewhere. The rifle spat its fifth shot, viciously assertive in the pause, a shot without echo, and from that lack of echo and the brief scream of the oncoming bullet, Reagan guessed that the sniper must be up on a roof top.

He seized advantage of the pause to fill his guns. While he was thumbing in fresh shells, he puzzled over the increasing sounds of commotion in the street. The men were arguing with one another, but in the confusion of tones he couldn't tell what the argument was about. Some of the men were evidently of a mind to make radical changes in the operation, for at the height of the hubbub he recognized Frank Tillander's voice raised in angry command.

"Back, you fools! Get back there, damn you, and—"

The rifle whipped two shots, hastened a flurry of running feet, and Tillander cursed. The sniper, too, had reloaded, was spending his loads discriminately. A man showed up at the open end of the alley. Reagan tilted a gun, held it. The man was tottering, too dazed to know where his knee-sagging legs were carrying him. Let him go. Save a shell. The sniper had checked that one out, among others. He heard somebody calling his name.

"Reagan! Come on, Reagan—I'm covering for you!"

The voice of Jim Carmack. The sniper. *Covering*, Reagan thought, *for me!* He disliked the phrase, distrusted it on principle. Too overpromising. No ordinary shooter, nor a gun wizard for that matter, could guarantee cover for a getaway from any number of armed men.

But Carmack's intentions were high, no question of that. Carmack was set to do his best against the whole town of Cochimi. His unlucky best. "Here goes!" Reagan muttered.

He sprinted up the alley and hit the street running. He heard Jim Carmack shout his name again in sudden, urgent warning, but he was going full pelt, putting everything into speed. A rapid glance brought him an impression that the street had emptied except for one dim figure coming downhill. Reason denied that a single rifle could have made the street safe for his exit. Then a shot exploded at him from a doorway, and men who had withdrawn to shelter yelled out at sight of him racing from the alley.

He fired on the run, snap-shooting at dark places most likely to contain threat. This upper end of the town, unlike the lower end, had few lights showing at this time of night, but there was a moon. Men came swarming out after him, darting from one shadow to the next, while Carmack, wherever he was, spent shot after shot in trying to drive them back. Reagan veered across the street, seeking a gap on that side, meanwhile keeping an eye on the dim figure coming downhill at a lumbering trot.

The dim figure promptly swung over to head him off. Moonlight dissipated the dimness, and the figure became Deputy Sheriff Heckels, shotgun leveled waist-high. Recognizing Reagan at the same instant that Reagan recognized him, Heckels uttered a syllable that sounded like, "Wup!" And, trotting faster, he rasped, "I told you Reagan—"

"Drop that scatter-gun!" Reagan said.

"I told you!" Heckels repeated pantingly. The shotgun both hammer ears cocked full, wobbled at Reagan. "You pull a breakout, I said, and I'll—"

"Drop it quick!"

"—I'll cut you in two!"

Reagan fired and jumped aside. He aimed charitably low, and Heckels fell lungingly as if striking a trip wire, the shotgun exploding both loads and flaying up dirt yards ahead of him, but his head took the brunt of the heavy fall. He lay motionless. Reagan said, "Sorry," and. "Damn it!" and ran on past.

He dodged into a gap between two unlighted houses, hav-

98

ing to slow down to make sure that the gap wasn't blocked at the rear end. Passing on through and emerging onto open ground, he found that he was at the edge of town and headed for the stand of cottonwoods. His pursuers had marked his direction of flight, he hadn't thrown them off, they were trampling hot on the trail.

Someone was actually gaining on him, some rash lightfoot, and he spun around to cut him down. But it was Jim Carmack, running like an Indian buck. Still covering for him, Jim slewed about-face and fired the rifle. "Keep going, Reagan!" he sang out. "I'll hold 'em off a minute!"

This was too much. No man had ever before had the temerity to make any such patronizing suggestion to Reagan. It crossed his mind that perhaps this young joker regarded him as past his prime, a bit over the age for fast capers. Hell's gall! "Look, you . . ." he growled.

He caught hold of the back of Jim's shirt, bunching it in a powerful fist, and slung him around. But then the thought came that maybe Jim was only trying to repay a favor in full measure, and all he said was, "Let's get to those horses . . ."

They ran together to the stand of cottonwoods. At the fringe they paused to blaze back and discourage too close a pursuit, and hurried on. Susan, holding three saddled horses, sent Reagan a quick smile as he and Jim joined her, but none of them spoke. They mounted up and set off at once. Susan was hatless. Her unbound hair tossed like a mane, and when they burst out from under the trees into the moonlight a cry arose:

"There they go—that girl's one of 'em! That girl—"

Thirteen

SOUTH ON THE edge of the valley Reagan raised his hand for a halt, and they drew in to listen for sounds of pursuing horsemen. "Nothing yet," Reagan said presently, "but they'll be along. Was it you," he asked Susan, "who let out that ungodly squawl?"

She nodded, rather proudly. "I fired the shots, too, before I screamed—to fool Heckels into coming out."

"It fooled me," Reagan admitted. "Fooled the Hi Jolly jokers, too. Tillander planned on doing pretty much the same thing at midnight. You beat him to it. Knocked his timing off. Were you shooting from the roofs, Carmack? You're a tomcat! Why did you yell at me as I left the alley?"

"I saw Heckels coming. Did you—"

"I had to drop him, yes. Tried not to kill him, but I don't know." The deputy sheriff had not yet written off to that Colorado lawyer for the Harby papers, Reagan reflected, but he didn't mention it to Susan and Jim. He said to them, "You were both spotted. Too bad. Wish it wasn't so."

His implied thanks reached them. Susan asked, "Does it mean we can't go back to the Gillespie ranch?"

"Nor any other place where they can find you," Reagan answered. "We're outlaws now for sure, the three of us! And if Heckels is dead—or even if he's only out of action—we can bet Tillander will take over until the district sheriff sends another deputy."

"You're right," Jim concurred. "You just don't do what we've done among us, and then quietly jog home! Especially us! Tillander will make the most of it. He'll push the hunt for us with every man he can call on. The law's on his side."

Another matter, which Reagan didn't bring up at the moment, was the fact that, in shooting down Heckels, he had undoubtedly alienated the cattle crowd. Heckels was the cowmen's sheriff; the cowmen were his lifelong friends and would lay the blame not only on the shooter but also

100

on the two who had aided in his getaway, lumping them together as a trio of disreputable hell-raisers.

He regretted having had to shoot Heckels. The deputy's bullheadedness had made the shooting necessary—it had been Heckels' life or his own—but he had known with cold clarity that it was a costly act the instant he fired. Its cost was disastrous for Susan—loss of friendly refuge, a shattering setback to her prospects of proving her identity and her claim to the Harby property, and a burden of condemnation. He sighed, wondering if Jim Carmack's hoodoo had transferred itself to him for a change and was operating in a big way on fresh blood.

"The question is," Jim said, "where do we go?"

Reagan didn't have any answer ready. He foresaw a relentless scouring of the country, all outbound routes closed, and no welcome for them at any ranch. A distant drumming made itself heard, and he threw his head up, listening, placing it northward, coming rapidly south. "Let's go!" he said. And again Jim asked, "Where?" And again Reagan had no answer.

There was nowhere left for them to go. Nowhere at all.

They rode without destination, impelled simply to shake off the oncoming posse. Their horses, borrowed by Jim, belonged in the valley, however, and took naturally to the familiar road homeward, unchecked. Reagan bent his thoughts to Mexico. He was picturing Susan in a mantilla, Spanish combs and all, when a single rider loomed up on the road ahead.

The rider reined his horse up broadside to the three fugitives, as though to dispute their right of way. Reagan bared a gun. Jim did the same, then said, "No, it's only Chris Gillespie—Bill Gillespie's young brother. Hi, Chris! You looking for something?"

"Looking for you!" came the reply. "Susan and you! Bill missed three horses, and you were both gone . . ."

He was young, Chris Gillespie, with a blatantly assertive manner that was obviously adopted to compensate for an inner uncertainty. He blinked startledly at Reagan, saw the condition of the horses, and comprehension dawned on his face. His pose of assurance struggled to rise again.

"Whyn't you tell me what you were up to?" he demanded of Jim aggrievedly. "I'da gone along, you know that! Do anything to help Susan—anything at all!"

It was a dead giveaway, his words, his tone in speaking

Susan's name, his look, everything. It was borne in upon Reagan that Susan exercised a pretty strong effect on males of all ages, whether she tried or not. That special quality of hers; not only her arresting beauty, but the heart-shaking promise breathed by passion underlying the modesty, by that piquant and challenging hint of—well—wantonness. A not yet awakened wantonness.

He said to Chris Gillespie, "You can do something to help now. A posse's after us. Tell 'em we took another road!"

"I can do better'n that!" the youth stated promptly. "You don't want"—with another look at Susan—"to go chasin' clear out o' the country. What you want is a hideaway. Follow me! I know this country sideways and backwards!"

"Handy for crabs," Reagan commented. But he shrugged assent. "Forward will do for now. Lead on!"

Chris Gillespie knew the country, all right, having been born and reared in it, and he led them due east off the road, making a considerable to-do of pickisg stony patches and covering their tracks. The earnest scurrying wearied Reagan, who didn't entertain any high opinion of the average man's tracking sense. This settled rangeland was well trodden. But he let it go. The youth was enjoying his importance.

Susan's horse developed a limp, slowing them, and it was Jim who suggested that the hither-and-yon progress might be exchanged for a straight line. Reluctantly Chris Gillespie shelved his role of wise scout and guided them directly to a stream he said was Little Papago, a branch of Big Papago. He turned upstream beneath a high bank of red clay, and, following him, they found him halted before a hole that had been cut into the bank.

"Long ago when I was a kid," he said from the heights of maturity, "some of us dug this for our secret cave. Nobody knows anything about it."

Dismounting, Reagan struck a match and inspected it. The entrance was smaller than the cave itself, which was crudely shored up with logs and boughs. He could discern no fresh marks on the floor. "Dry, anyhow," he observed. "Nobody seems to have been here for a year or two. Boys' secret club house, um? Bet you snuck here to get out of chores!"

"Well, you know how kids are."

"I seem to remember, now you remind me."

"It's all yours," Chris said grandly. "You'll be wanting grub and stuff." He pinched his lower lip between thumb

102

and forefinger, plainly worrying over that problem. "Can't let Susan go hungry!"

"Not to mention us! But you better not—"

"Be back in the morning...!" He reined off and was gone.

"Impetuous," Jim murmured. "We should have warned him to keep his mouth shut. Guess he will, though. Think this'll do, Reagan? Safe enough?"

"It'll have to do for tonight. We'll take turns staying awake." Reagan stripped the saddles off his and Susan's horses. He examined the lame foot and pried out a piece of flint. He carried the saddle blankets into the cave. "We'll let you stand first watch, Carmack."

"Sleep well," Jim said politely. He squatted at the mouth of the cave. "It's sure quiet. I'll just sit here and listen. Wake you up if I hear anything."

Chris Gillespie showed up in the morning with a bunch of young cowboys as wild as himself.

They came roaring up the riverbank like a troop of green cavalry pitching its first charge, full of glory and high resolution to do or die for a grand cause, with no more discretion than a stampeding herd of two-year bulls. Reagan reared up, guns out and cocked, and Jim was fast along with him. Susan grabbed the rifle.

"G'mornin', folks!" Chris sang out, meaning it obviously for Susan, and all the troop echoed his greeting to her while proudly eying her. She was the shining star of their glorious cause. Pretty sickening, Reagan thought it.

It transpired that they were all-out to place Susan upon her rightful throne. The Rocking H. Nothing less would do. They were avid for it. Avid for her, too, every one of them, although they tried not to show it too blatantly. They were so young, so impressionable, so infatuated with lovely Susan. Their queen.

"Look, you—" Reagan began, and then cut off what he had begun to call them.

He sighed heavily. They were a flock of unruly cockerels, spoiling for mischief and excitement. Full of daring. He remembered that they had spent all their lives here in this isolated community. Their wordly knowledge was based largely on hearsay. Action was their strong point; any kind of action. Cogitation was to them a sign of enfeebling age, if not of timidity, and caution they scorned.

Reagan recalled a pungent line he had picked up some-

103

where in his past: "He jests at scars, that never felt a wound."

In the midst of their noisy babble he gathered the fact that Deputy Sheriff Heckels was believed to have suffered a concussion when he landed on his head in the street. The bullet through his leg had not been too damaging, but at last report the deputy was still unconscious, and there was talk of a vigilante committee forming under Frank Tillander's leadership.

But that carried little weight with the young champions. They were frothing at the bit, bubbling with wild plans for securing Susan her rights, the wilder the better and the devil take care of the consequences. "What we should do," Chris Gillespie declared fiercely, "is to take the Rocking H right now! Just dash in"—he made a sweeping gesture that caused his horse to shy startledly under him—"and take it! Possession is nine points o' the law, ain't it?"

"You asking?" Reagan queried him. Giving it thought, however, he saw some merit in the proposal. It was a move of stark desperation, of course, and would have to be modified from Chris's foolhardy conception of it. But the situation was as desperate as it could be.

As a hideout for any length of time the cave was hopeless. Even if Chris and his pals could be relied upon not to spill the secret accidentally, their behavior would soon arouse suspicion and anybody could follow their bunched tracks. There was no place else to hide, so . . .

"I want to scout the Rocking H first," Reagan said, "and get an idea of the layout."

Jim Carmack blinked at him. "You mean you're thinking of trying it?" he muttered incredulously. "Man, you're as crazy as them! If we took the outfit, we couldn't hold it!"

Reagan shook his head. "You can't tell. These cockerels crave action. They'll get it one way or other, no matter what we do. All right, we'll give 'em a taste of it! Let 'em in the game, let 'em get their feet wet, and then maybe their folks—the cattle crowd—will pile in, if only to save 'em!"

"Would you actually use these green fledglings?" Jim demanded. "Against Tillander's thugs?"

"Why, yes," Reagan drawled. "This black day I'd use rosy cherubs and pure-white angels, if I saw one slim chance out of the jackpot we're in!"

"*Slim* is right!"

"Sure! But I don't see anything else, do you? Let's go take a squint at that outfit, anyhow!"

The difficulty with Reagan's reconnoiter of the Rocking H lay in ridding the young cowboys of their notion to stage a raid there and then. They were dazzled with the vision of a headlong charge, Susan as audience. As hotly competitive as Indian warriors, every one of them yearned to outdo the rest in some act of splendid madness. Reagan managed to restrain them with strong and forceful language, which cost him considerable popularity. Their looks informed him that he was a spoilsport and very likely a broken-down has-been whose nerve was worn out. Past performances were not always sufficient recommendation in the gunfighting trade. A hot-shot *could* fizzle out.

Surveying the Rocking H from the distant sweep of hills, seeing it for the first time by daylight, he observed for himself what Amiel Harby had done with the money, the hard-earned money he has stolen from his partners after betraying them in Texas: poured it all, and more, into this place.

And he could understand Frank Tillander's cold-blooded murder of Harby. Vengeance had not been the only motive. This ranch filled the answer. This jewel of a ranch. He could appreciate Frank Tillander's determination to keep it at any cost. Frank hungered for prestige, possessions. Nothing could ever satisfy that hunger like a fine ranch. In his own eyes it gave him nobility, topmost success. It made him superior, a range aristocrat. Nothing less would do.

"It's a cattleman's heaven!" Reagan murmured. The old stirring rose powerfully within him. He set his mind to lining up cold facts. A plan, previously half formed, began taking shape.

There were perhaps six men on the ranch, he calculated. Hardly more, for Frank Tillander would certainly be using every man he could spare in scouring the country for the fugitives and blocking all routes of escape. Six armed men, gunmen, could cut this flock of unseasoned lads to pieces in short order. On the other hand . . .

"No!" Jim muttered, guessing at Reagan's thoughts. "We can't do it! Can't risk these young'uns. They don't know what it's like! If we get 'em hurt—just one of 'em—we'll have the whole cattle crowd out for our blood! And they'll be right, too! These are their young'uns, and we've got no business—"

"You talk like Heckels!" Reagan growled at him. "They're dead set on mischief. My idea is to steer them off. At the same time, they can do a little job for us—and without getting hurt."

"How?"

"Diversionary tactics, army men call it." Reagan turned to the restless cowboys and raised his voice. "All right, fellers, now listen ..."

Fourteen

THAT EVENING, WAITING with Jim and Susan on a slope overlooking the Rocking H ranch house, Reagan reviewed his plan in a mood of increasing unsureness.

It was the waiting, he tried to tell himself, that caused his pessimism. The waiting, and the difference between sunshine and moonlight. What appeared possible in the bright blaze of day changed aspect under the cold moon. He regretted bringing Susan along on this last-chance venture, although common sense said that she could not have been left anywhere. No place was safe for her.

"What time do they show up?" Jim asked him.

He shook his head. "I didn't set any special time. Can't, that kind of job."

While they listened to the small sounds of the night, straining to pick out a noise above others, their eyes kept straying to the lighted windows of the ranch house. "Think they can do it without a bobble?" Jim murmured.

"How the devil do I know?" Reagan snapped irritably, and then was angry at his edginess and at himself for showing it. Nerves. Maybe the cocksure cowboys were right in their unspoken suspicion about him. Maybe he was slipping, a has-been. He shook off the thought, knowing too well its destructive power.

His plan was simple. The cowboys were to gather up two or three hundred head of cattle belonging to their own folks, and drive the herd through Rocking H range after dark, within earshot of the house. Then they were to abandon the herd and quietly go home. That was all.

It struck the youths as pretty tame. They realized that the purpose of it was to lure the Rocking H crew out to investigate what would sound like a rustling operation, but it didn't satisfy their craving for high excitement. Just a job of work. However, Reagan had finally talked them into agreeing to do it, and off they trooped, disappointed.

From what Reagan could figure after hours of watching, there were only five men on the place, and Frank Tillander was not one of them. Frank, he supposed, was either staying in town or was out with the hunters. The five men wore their guns and kept horses saddled in the yard, plainly prepared for emergencies at any time of day or night. Just before sundown Felisa Plevin had driven in alone, in the box buggy. She had gone into the house, evidently to stay the night, for one of the men took the bugggy over to the wagon shed and stripped the team.

The presence of the woman created an extra problem, particularly if she had her pistol with her and took a whim to use it. Still, Reagan reflected, she might be of some value as a hostage . . .

"That 'em?" Jim muttered. A minute later he exclaimed, "Can't be! Sounds like a real herd! Coming this way, though!"

Reagan nodded. "More'n two or three hundred head in that bunch. Maybe our lads can't count. Oh well—just so they push 'em this far."

The heavy rumble suddenly increased, accompanied by sullen bawling. Soon, like streams in the moonlight, the cattle could be seen swarming down the folds of the north hills. That far off, the animals made a strangely unreal sight, their tossing horns seeming to writhe like bone-pale snakes above the steaming bodies, and when their eyes caught the moonlight they glared reflecting it red.

"Pushing 'em too fast!" Jim commented.

"Never mind that," Reagan said. "Look!"

Five men ran out into the Rocking H ranch yard and clustered for a moment, staring northward. The door of the house was flung open and Felisa Plevin stood outlined against the light within. The men, shouting something to her, ran to the saddled horses. They hurriedly tightened up cinches, mounted, and rode out of the yard. Felisa Plevin gazed after them and withdrew into the house, leaving the door open.

"Now's when we move in, Carmack!" Reagan said. "Stay close behind us, Susan!"

They rode down and circled the yard and tied their horses behind the wagon shed. The noise of the oncoming cattle made caution unnecessary. They walked around to the front of the house, and Reagan, entering first, looked about him at a comfortably furnished living room. He passed on through it and two more rooms, tracking a homey sound, and came upon Felisa Plevin in the kitchen.

She was standing at the cookstove, her back to him, slowly stirring the contents of a saucepan. For her to be engaged in such a commonplace task appeared a trifle incongruous; a witch's caldron would hardly have surprised him. Without taking her attention off the saucepan she asked, "That you Floyd? What's the trouble out there?"

"Good evening   Mrs. Plevin!" he said, and she whirled around in a flash, the saucepan held to fling the scalding contents full at his face. He ducked, for the sake of his eyes throwing up a shielding hand. "Don't do it!" he rapped. "I've never shot a woman—but that's not to say I wouldn't, to save my eyes!"

"I believe you would!' She lowered the saucepan. Then, catching sight of Susan, who with Jim had followed him in, she started to raise it again. Her face was a dead mask.

Reagan brought his raised hand down, his fingers snapping around her wrist. "Smells like good stew," he said. "Serve us! On plates! Before I take my belt to you!"

"I'm not afraid of any man!" she sneered.

"That might be your trouble." Keeping hold of her wrist, he took the saucepan from her and set it back on the stove. "A hard woman—a domineering woman . . ."

He never finished the remark. A shrill yell cut through the thunder of the passing cattle; a boy's yell, not of exuberance but of alarm. Gunshots began cracking. A horse squealed its death agony, and somebody—likely its young rider—screamed in sheer panic. The shots continued, punctuating the hoarse shouting of men exchanging orders. Another youthful yell sounded, and another.

"Oh, my God!" Jim uttered is as in prayer. "They stayed with the herd! The fools—the crazy young fools! They'll be slaughtered! Reagan—"

"We've got to help them! We must!' The statement came from Susan, and both men stared at her as if she had suddenly changed personalities with Felisa Plevin.

"You're staying here till we get back," Reagan told her. "Bar the door after us, and shoot if anybody tries to break in. As for you, Mrs. Plevin . . ." He pushed the woman quickly into a closet before she realized what he was up to, and shut the door, bracing it with a chair under the doorknob. "Don't let her out,' he warned Susan, "or you're liable to find yourself in the stew!"

The cattle were stampeding. They had not been shaped up as anything like a trail herd to begin with. They had been choused around, pushed too fast, and the gunshots had completed their upset. A mob of them was boiling off southward, while others milled about, fighting mad, hooking at anything in their path. Dust clogged the air, and in the wild confusion nothing definite could be distinguished.

A rider careened by, and Reagan couldn't tell whether it was boy or man, friend or enemy, or Jim Carmack. The last he had seen of Jim, a crazed cow was charging him, and his horse appeared to be turning cart wheels. Bad luck.

Reagan could hear no further shooting, but occasionally a faint shouting reached him through the din, from which direction it was difficult to decide. All it told him was that the Rocking H men were still busy, though it was possible that they were busy extricating themselves from the stampede. His horse reared, and he thought that he was going to have trouble with it, for the animal was wrought up. Then a figure rose groggily almost from under the stirrups, and, peering down closely into its white face, he recognized one of Chris Gillespie's young pals.

"You hurt?" he asked.

The youth moved his head dazedly to and fro. "Dunno, mister! But Chris . . ."

"Where?"

"Cows all around us. Stampeded. He's"—the youth gestured widely southward—"right in it there, somewhere! His horse bolted with him. No-good horse, that china-eye pinto, I always told him . . ."

"Any other of you fellers hurt?"

"Dunnno. We stuck with the herd. They came up shootin'. Cheez! Shootin' like—"

"Where's your horse?"

"Dunno. Threw me."

"Get another here from Rocking H and make your way home, fast!" Reagan reined around and spurred his horse to a flat run southward.

When he began passing stragglers of the stampede it gave him some hope that the stampede itself might have dissipated, broken up into bunches, allowing young Chris to pull out unharmed. He soon abandoned that hope, hearing a roar ahead. The bulk of the herd stayed bunched. Worse than bunched, for a horseman trying to outride them; the maddened cattle plunged blindly onward in the deadly half-moon formation that gave trail drovers bad dreams. The stronger cattle, forging foremost, formed the prongs of the half-moon, and if nothing stopped them they closed in. A man trapped in the middle . . .

He drew abreast of the stampede, passed the leaders, and, twisting for a backward look he spied a lone rider in the black ruck of the cattle. The rider's right arm rose and fell repeatedly, lashing his horse, a pinto pony. In the jerky rise

110

and fall of that punishing arm there was panic, horror of the madly relentless hoofs reaching behind, and the shining, clacking horns.

That boy, Reagan thought pityingly, *is scared witless.*

He swung over, well into the course of the onrushing brutes, trusting his horse to keep its footing and its sense. In the hope of splitting their solid front he fired a gun empty over them. It hadn't the slightest effect. They were spooked blind, running with heads low and horns outthrust, and would run straight onward like that until some obstruction turned them or exhaustion beat them to a standstill.

He checked the gait of his horse, forcing it to lose ground. The animal, having sense, fought against dropping back into that terrifying maw, compelling him to saw reins on the bridle bit as a drastic recourse until the two prongs of the herd came up level. He was now in the middle, deafened by the roar of cattle, feeling the heat generated by their bodies, but he was still a length ahead of young Chris. The pinto pony labored, wind-spent.

Reagan made his split-second calculations, hauled up hard, and reached out his arm as the failing pinto bobbed alongside. Chris kicked his stirrups loose, dropped his reins, and when he came swaying over to him Reagan dragged him from the saddle. The lad was not heavy. Reagan held onto him and gave his horse its head.

Gradually they drew forward. The horse bore its double load strongly, but for how long it could maintain its speed was a question. Reagan edged it over to the left, watching for a chance to pull out. The horse knew his mind and, racing out front, it darted across the path of the leaders and cleared them by a narrow margin. It didn't have time to dodge a steer plunging along the outside fringe.

Reagan never even saw the brute. It came up on a tangent from behind and rammed the horse on the flanks, and Reagan spun head-over-heels backward, the jar nearly breaking his neck. The second jar came from hitting the ground, where he rolled like a ball before he fetched up against a rock.

Some little time later he raised his buzzing head off the ground and took stock. All was quiet except for a low rumble dying off in the distance. His horse had scrambled up and bolted. He felt himself all over for broken bones, then thought of Chris and looked for him.

Chris lay face up, arms spread. His breathing was his only sign of life. "A fine damn' mess!" Reagan muttered, inspecting him. Though only his cuts and scratches showed blood, the lad was as limp as an empty sack. No telling what internal injuries he might have sustained, and how dangerous it might be to move him; yet he couldn't be left lying out here.

"A fine damn' mess!" Reagan muttered again. He picked Chris up, paused to get his bearings, and resigned himself to tramping back afoot to the Rocking H.

Fifteen

THEY WERE IN the ranch yard: Jim Carmack and a youth and a body wrapped in a blanket. The youth sat bowed with his face buried in his hands, shivering. He barely roused to look up when Reagan trudged in, an arm supporting Chris, who had revived sufficiently along the way to use his legs in an uncertain fashion.

The front door of the house hung ajar, and a light burned in there although the sun was coming up. "Susan?" Reagan barked at Jim. He let Chris stagger on unaided to the porch steps and slump down on them. The sitting youth got up weakly and joined him. He was the same one Reagan had almost ridden over at the start of the stampede. He began mumbling to Chris, and pointed a trembling finger at the blanket-wrapped body.

Jim had given Reagan no reply, merely gazing at him stonily. Reagan stepped to the body, and nearly recoiled. The face was uncovered, unrecognizable, battered to a bloody mass.

"Is this—"

"One of the young'uns, yes!" Jim said tonelessly. "He's Charlie Magee, grandson of old Eph Magee. So Dave tells me. That's Dave there—Dave Conlin. The Rocking H hands did it. Two or three of them got hurt in last night's mixup. It made 'em ugly. They put their boots to the kid!"

"Where were you?" Reagan demanded.

"I was busy." The words came bitingly. "Busy helping some of the other young'uns get home. That's how the Rocking H hands got hurt. Then I lost my horse. You're not the only one who had to walk. I only got here half an hour ago. Dave's told me what happened."

"Well?"

"They caught Dave here, trying for a horse. They'd already caught Charlie. Susan stood them off from getting in the house. They beat Dave up some. Charlie took a rock and hit one, and they started in on him. They kicked him till Susan couldn't stand his screaming any more. She opened the door and gave up. They put her on a horse and took her away!"

113

"To Cochimi?"

"Maybe," Jim said sparely. "They needed their hurts doctored. But who knows?" Then his pent-up fury burst, and he rasped, "You and your diversionary tactics! Your plan to take this ranch! It's all you've had in mind—this ranch! For yourself! To get it you'd sacrifice anybody! Even Susan! You're no better than Tillander! Two of a kind! Gun slingers out for yourselves and hell take everybody else! Longriders on the make . . .

Reagan gave him time to run it all off. He couldn't blame Carmack for his outburst, knowing how he felt about Susan. He half wished that he too had somebody to curse besides himself for the calamity. He said wearily at last, "All right, all right, let it go!" A thought occurred to him, and he asked Dave Conlin, "Did the Plevin woman leave with them?"

The youth eyed him vacantly. "Dunno. I didn't see no woman. 'Cept Susan."

"What? No . . ." Reagan took quick strides into the house and on through to the kitchen. The chair remained exactly as he had placed it, jammed beneath the knob of the closet door, bracing it shut.

A curious hesitancy possessed him to tap on the door and call, "Mrs. Plevin?"

There was no answer from within, not a sound. He jerked the chair away and opened the door. Felisa Plevin tumbled out and fell at his feet. Her face was bluish, the hue of suffocation. He had not noticed, when he shoved her in, how very shallow was the closet, how it had no window or any other means of ventilation, or how tightly the door fitted.

"Lord forgive me!" he muttered. "Now I've killed a woman!"

Jim Carmack, following him in, gave him a strange stare and knelt beside the woman. Presently he rose, saying, "Let's take her out in the fresh air."

They carried her out between them to the front porch, where it was Jim who worked over her while Reagan went and hitched the team up to the buggy. Reagan believed Felisa Plevin was stone dead, but when he drove the buggy up to the front of the house she was making snuffling sounds. "Charlie's alive, but Dave says it's too far to drive him home to the Magee ranch," Jim told him. "Chris thinks his brother's place is best. It's the nearest. Dave'll go there, too. And we'll have to take Mrs. Plevin."

"We better pick up a couple of horses here. It'll be a

114

load for the rig." Reagan shook his head. "Damn! Two banged-up boys, a nearly dead one, and a woman gasping for life!"

"And Susan . . ." Jim straightened his shoulders "Quite a night's work!"

"I'm not proud of it," Reagan said.

"Nor me," Jim admitted.

Chris Gillespie's elder brother, Bill, had the straight mouth and severe eyes of a man able without difficulty to distinguish wrong from right. He let it be known that Chris's lapse into rapscallion mischief was a natural result of idleness. Hard work was the salvation of the young, as proved by himself, and unprofitable pleasure was an invention of the devil.

"But you're to blame!" he informed Reagan. "You've done more harm in a few days—more havoc than any man should do in a lifetime and expect to escape the penalty! Fighting and killing! Breaking jail and shooting up the town! Wounding my brother-in-law, the sheriff! Leading my brother and his silly friends astray—"

"They were straying pretty wild when I met them," Reagan interposed, but Gillespie ignored it.

"Oh, I'll do my duty!" he stated. "I'll get the doctor out here. I'll send word to Charlie Magee's folks. But I'll do nothing for you, nor for Carmack! The law is hunting you, and rightly so! I'll not have any wanted outlaws on my place! You've got to go!"

His wife seconded him. She was sorry to hear about Susan, she said, for she had liked her when she stayed here, but she had faith that the law would protect Susan, and, if not, then justice would eventually prevail. Some facts you simply had to accept. Mrs. Gillespie did not, however, accept with equal philosophy the fact that Reagan had shot her father in the leg and spilled him on his head in the street. That was a very serious matter.

Felisa Plevin, having recovered in a malevolent humor, snapped, "I'm going to Cochimi! These good Gillespies turn my stomach! You going to stop me, Reagan?"

He considered her for a moment before shaking his head. "Are you able to drive the buggy?"

"I paid for that flossy turnout!"

"Guess you can handle it, then."

They left the Gillespie place, Felisa Plevin driving the buggy, Reagan and Jim riding the horses they had bor-

115

rowed from the Rocking H. After they cleared the ranch, Reagan rode forward and bent over the buggy. "Pull up!" he told Felisa.

"What for?"

"Pull up, I said!"

When she had drawn the team to halt, he said to her, "You know Frank figures to get rid of you, don't you? Throw you out? Maybe kill you?"

"He'll throw me out if he's got your Susan Harby, yes! If I don't kill her first!"

"He'd kill you sure for that!"

She was silent, frowning at the team. "I learned one thing in that closet. Learned I don't want to live without Frank. He's rotten, but I've helped to make him that way. We had a bad row yesterday. Yes, he wants rid of me. As long as Susan Harby's anywhere around, he'll always want rid of me. What can I do?"

"Help me," Reagan said, "and I'll help you."

She looked up at him with a faint, wry smile. "Like we did before?"

"Same terms, anyhow. Drive on into town and find out what you can. Try to meet us—um, better leave that to you, and *we'll* try."

"I'll be driving alone back out to the ranch again tonight, I suppose. About sundown or a bit later."

He nodded. "We'll look for you somewhere along the road."

Her faint smile twisted. "Don't trust me much, do you?"

"Should I?"

"You should."

"All right."

They watched her drive on. Jim asked, "*Do* you trust her?"

"Yes," Reagan said. "Yes, I think I do."

They waited in the chaparral near the valley turnoff, watching the road from Cochimi. The long day's heat was lessening with the low sinking of the sun, but in the thick brush it still hung stifling and the two men sucked pebbles in place of water. Their horses stood drooping dispiritedly.

The sun touched the horizon. Jim murmured, "No sign of her yet!"

"She said about sundown," Reagan reminded him, "or a bit later."

"Yeah, That's what she said."

116

"Shut up!"

They were proddy, their nerves raw from waiting, from skulking all day in the chaparral, worrying, wondering if this was a mistake. The woman might be laughing at them. Or laying a trap for them. As time dragged on, Reagan could imagine her giving out the word of their whereabouts. Despite her denial, she had reason to carry a grudge.

The sun dipped, was gone,, and soon the golden afterglow faded to steel blue. "Still no sign of her!" said Jim.

"Shut up, I tell you! I've got eyes!"

Also, she was a vengeful woman. Vindictive and hard, domineering. Her moments of self-revelation in the kitchen closet wouldn't really change her nature. Too set in her pattern. No softness there.

The brief dusk deepened to darkness. Too early for moonlight, they could not see the road. "She's not coming!" Jim said. "She's—"

"You're a liar," Reagan interrupted him. "What's that I hear?"

They listened. "I was never so happy to be called a liar," Jim said. "I hear it too! Let's go!"

"Let's go easy," Reagan said. "She just *might* have a posse somewhere by!"

"I thought you trusted her!"

"Me? Don't ever trust a female like her!"

Now that the strain of waiting was passed, they worked together as team, with full confidence in each other and not a thought of criticism. They trotted their horses to the turnoff, Reagan taking one side of the road, Jim the other. The box buggy approached at a spanking gait, too fast for safety in the dark, brass gig-lamps unlighted, and when it drew near enough Reagan called, "Haul up, Mrs. Plevin, here we are!"

She pulled in between them, handling the team strongly. "You sound pretty easy, Mr. Reagan!" she said.

"Why not?" He reined his horse alongside the buggy. "Knew you'd show up. Alone, of course." He keyed his ears for sounds of trailing horsemen.

"Had a bad day?"

"Not a bit of it. Rested."

"Liar!" she said coolly. "I can guess how it was." she tied the lines and leaned forward. "The cattle crowd's up in arms over young Charlie Magee. Heckels is recovering, but Frank went ahead and formed a vigilante committee—his own men, of course. They pushed some of the cowmen around, and there's bad feeling. So, Frank's pulled his men back into the Hi Jolly to avoid further trouble. And that's how it stands. The cowmen are sore at him, on account of young Charlie. It's opened their eyes to the kind of men he's got working for him. Just because their boys ran some of their cows through Rocking H was—"

"Susan?" Reagan cut in.

"—no reason to nearly kick the kid to death, they maintain," she continued, deliberately disregarding his question. "But it's you they blame for that prank. They'd like to lynch you for getting their boys in trouble! And I don't think Heckels would do anything to stop them! In fact, it would let off their steam. You'd make a handy scapegoat for everybody, Mr. Longrider Reagan!"

"Susan?" he demanded again.

"Oh, her?" Felisa Plevin feigned an elaborate unconcern. "Where d'you suppose she is?"

"The Hi Jolly?"

"Where else? Deck Floyd and his riders took her straight there to Frank. Deck's foreman of Rocking H, remember, and it was him did the kicking. The cowmen want his hide for it, but all they do is mill around talking. Talk-talk-talk! You should hear old Eph Magee sounding off! Frank's laughing up his sleeve at them. He knows they'll simmer down finally and go back home to work—still talking! He's made himself the kingpin of Cochimi," she said with bitter pride, "and he's safe there in the Hi Jolly. Where else would he hold your Susan Harby? Where else *could* he hold her?"

"Upstairs?"

"Yes—but don't count on me helping you this time! I don't have free run in the Hi Jolly anymore. Frank's as good as thrown me out. The buzzard! The bone-picking buzzard . . . !"

Reagan spoke across her to Jim. "You ready for town?"

"Sure!" Jim said.

"It'll be tough—tougher than any jackpot you've ever been in! Or me! The whole town, the cowmen, Frank Tillander's mob—and just us two—"

"I'm ready, Lew."

"Okay, Jim."

The woman called, "Hey, you bullheads!" But they were already spurring up the dark road to Cochimi.

Sixteen

THE MEN WHO congregated down along the low end of the main street, in shadowy groups, shared one thing in common with those inside the Hi Jolly: they were keeping quiet. Even old Eph Magee, stalking from group to group, denouncing the brutal beating of his young grandson, held his voice down to a complaining rumble. The whole town was hushed, and the Hi Jolly did not flaunt its brightest lights, nor did anyone play the piano.

Returning from cautiously scouting the town on foot, Reagan said to Jim, "You'd think they were all in mourning!"

"I guess nobody wants to risk a flare-up," Jim muttered. Their rendezvous was the rubbish-littered yard behind the saddle shop, and he kept his gaze fixed on a small lighted window upstairs in the rear of the Hi Jolly.

Reagan nodded. Nobody wanted a flare-up. These solid citizens and cattlemen had let Frank Tillander get away with murder, let him and his cutthroat mob take over their town —and what finally had aroused them was the beating of a boy. It was scarcely logical, though understandable.

But they were not so stirred up as to take action, because action was irrevocable, a step into a blazing showdown, and none of them cared to shoulder the responsibility. On the contrary, they were treading on tiptoe, avoiding making any overt move that might spark off an explosion. They would spend their feelings in talk and go home with a sense of defeat. Frank Tillander, too, was being careful, but next time he would know that he didn't need to worry. He'd have the Indian sign on them.

"How'd you get up on that roof?" Reagan asked Jim, motioning toward the saddle shop.

"Climbed up the corner of the new part at the back. It's got some boards sticking out that haven't been trimmed off." Jim moved with sudden impatience. "Look, I'm not going to wait for something to happen that's not going to happen!"

"That window, um?" Reagan said softly. He glanced at the lighted window upstairs in the Hi Jolly. "Well, that's most likely where she is, all right. And a man or two standing guard below it!"

119

"Three! I spied 'em while you were gone. I could've dropped one, maybe two."

"Noise! Be a dozen more there before she could get out!"

"I know, but we can't——"

"No, hold it till something happens."

"What?"

"I'm not quite sure," Reagan said, moving off, "but it might be something to do with a blue wagon. Guess I'll call on the deputy sheriff..."

He climbed to the roof of the saddle shop and crossed onto the jail, and there looked at the little square of light on the second floor of the Hi Jolly. Jim Carmack would need some luck to get Susan out of there. It occurred to him to wonder why he was letting Jim take on that job, and giving himself this other task—a thankless and suicidal task. The answer that came most readily to him was that getting Susan out of the Hi Jolly wasn't enough. It would do nothing toward securing her claim to Rocking H. She would never gain her rights while Frank kept his health.

It wasn't completely the answer, but he accepted it and looked no more at the lighted window.

The chopped hole in the jail roof had not yet been repaired. Nor would it be, he supposed, until Deputy Sheriff Heckels became able to do it himself. Civic pride required a permanent and responsible citizenry, and Cochimi, with its sorry preponderance of fly-by-night dodgers, had fallen far into slipshod ways. Carefully Reagan lowered himself through the hole and dropped soundlessly onto his toes inside the short corridor of the jail. The door between the jail and sheriff's office hung open. He saw Heckels' blocky figure in the unlighted office, standing motionless at the wrecked front window, and he walked forward and spoke to him with quiet distinctness:

"Good evening, Sheriff!"

Deputy Sheriff Heckels was supporting himself with a stick. As he had done once before, he now showed again a surprising aplomb. "Good evening, Mr. Reagan," he said formally, turning from the window. "I've been sort of expecting you."

And then, harshly, "I've been looking at my town! At my old friends down there in the street! They're licked, d'you know? So'm I! If we make a move, we're dead! And all due to you, damn you!"

"Why me?" Reagan asked him, but he knew the answer and it was forthcoming.

"You've brought it to a head! Using those kids! I knew you'd do it if you broke loose. Do anything to get your way! A longrider, here today and gone tomorrow, hell mend your tracks! I was holding my town under some control, some law and order—"

"By meeting the thugs halfway!"

"Call it what you like, I—"

"There's a girl locked up in the Hi Jolly! A good, decent girl—Susan Harby—prisoner! What're you and your fine friends doing about it? Nothing!"

"Poor young Charlie Magee's like to die, and old Eph and the crowd want Deck Floyd for it! Tillander won't give him up to 'em. Or don't dare. They'd settle for you if they could get hold of you!"

Reagan spat savagely. "I'm a longrider—all right, but I can teach you how to take hold and how to hold tight! D'you want to stew here, or d'you want your town?"

"You lamed me—" Heckels began, but Raegan cut him short.

"One leg! You got another leg! You got two hands! What the hell more d'you want—cavalry and a gunboat? I'll show you."

He strode out to the blue wagon at the side of the jail. The ground sheet containing the supply of hay still hung beneath the high body. He struck a match and tossed it into the hay. He kicked the chocks out from under the wheels, and shoved. The wagon moved, rolling ponderously backward on the downhill grade, and Deputy Sheriff Heckels came limping out of his office, shouting, "Reagan! You maniac! Stop—"

Reagan couldn't have stopped the heavy wagon now if he had wanted to, and he didn't intend to try. He let it trundle past him, slowly gathering momentum. The iron-thimbled end of the wagon tongue came dragging by like a tail, and he lifted it and walked with it. Soon he was trotting, then running. Yells everywhere broke the pall of silence that had hung over the town.

Spouting flame and trailing hay sparks, the tall blue wagon careened downhill, rocking into the deep ruts of the street. Reagan found the pace too fast, and the heat thrown back at his face was becoming unbearable. The body of the wagon was burning. Then fire suddenly swept right over the canvas top, and he flung himself down on the wagon tongue

121

and rode it flattened on his stomach. Above the noise he heard shouts of alarm. Somewhere close ahead shots cracked.

He couldn't see the Hi Jolly, or anything else, for the smoke pouring over him. Blind calculation had to be his guide. A twisting lurch told him that he was meeting the bend in the street where daily traffic had to turn aside because of the Hi Jolly's protruding front. He had forgotten to take those ruts into account.

On their ringed and movable axle the front wheels of the backward-running wagon were tracking in the ruts, and the tongue, fixed to the axle, jerked under him like a live thing trying to sling him off. He was going to swerve around the curve and roll on uselessly to the bottom of the grade...

"While everybody takes pot shots at me!"

He slid off the tongue and threw his weight against it, using it as an unwieldy tiller to steer the wagon. The cramped wheels shuddered, jumped the ruts. The wagon slewed hard over, and at the capsize point its foremost wheels crunched into a boardwalk and it seemed to leap, to rear up like the bow of a ship driven aground under full sail. The next instant there was a mighty crash.

The wagon plowed on with prolonged crashings, dragging Reagan through a welter of wreckage before he thought to let go. He skidded into a table and some chairs, and lay shaking his head to clear it, bits of burning canvas floating down about him. Becoming aware of a need to move, he clawed free of the tangle of barroom furniture.

"On the mark!" he muttered. "Hit it dead on the mark!"

The wagon, having smashed through the windows and wall of the Hi Jolly, had knocked the bar askew, caromed off, and rammed into the side wall. It had made a shambles of the barroom. Smoke was filling the place, and spreading flames threatened to complete its destruction very soon. The wagon was a roaring torch.

Men ran out through the gaping hole in the wall. They cursed, jostling one another. The stentorian voice of old Eph Magee rose bellowing at them: "Lay down them guns—lay 'em down! Hey—there's Deck Floyd...!" A shot set off a flurry of gunfire that lasted only seconds, then Heckels was shouting, "Hold it! Hold it, everybody!"

A tall, gangling figure darted across the barroom. Reagan called, "Frank—"

Without stopping, Frank Tillander twisted, pistol in hand, and fired in the direction of Reagan's voice. Reagan jerked a broken chair from around his leg and flung it at him. A downdraft of smoke swirled between them. Losing sight of Frank, Reagan made for the door marked "Rooms."

The burning wagon stood within six feet of the door, canted over toward it on the hub of a collapsed wheel. Its irons glowed red hot, and the floor beneath it was a pool of flame. The boards of the wall buckled, turning brown. Hot resin dripped from the pine ceiling. Frank Tillander was trying to reach the door. He had one hand up to shield his eyes from the heat, the other outstretched toward the doorknob.

Reagan called to him again, "Frank!"

Frank Tillander retreated two steps from the door, swiftly, and turned with a movement of savage impatience. He was bareheaded. His fair hair hung lankly over glaring blue eyes. In the firelight his pale face took on a sunken cast, like the lipless grin of a skeleton. He crouched, launched himself at Reagan, and Reagan saw then that the man was grinning in a frenzy of rage.

Reagan met him with a straight-arm punch. It jolted Frank upright, but in his crouch he had snatched up a broken plank and he swung it sidelong like an ax in both hands. Reagan took the blow on his left shoulder. He had reason then to remember Frank Tillander's tremendous strength and quickness, for it knocked him off balance and the next swipe drove him sprawling. He floundered on the floor, suddenly realizing that his left arm was numbed, that Frank had the upper hand.

Frank's laugh sounded thin and ragged. "Burn! Burn here alive, damn you!" He struck down at Reagan's face.

Reagan raked his shins with a boot heel while squirming aside, and kicked at his middle. Frank flinched, then swung, missing by inches, striking the floor beyond Reagan's head, but the force of the blow broke off part of the plank, and the edge of the remaining length hit Reagan high on the forehead. Dimly Reagan heard him repeat:

"Burn here alive, damn you!"

Struggling to rise, Reagan discovered that all his effort was going into rolling his head. His sense cleared and he pushed himself up on his good arm. He saw the fiery remains of the wagon capsize as the floor caved in beneath it. He watched Frank rush in and chop at the warped door with the piece of plank. Frank was still intent upon getting through that door and upstairs.

123

Reagan said, "Frank, don't do that! It's no use!"

Frank Tillander didn't glance his way, evidently not hearing him, believing that he had settled with him. He did back away, though, because broad patches of charred black suddenly streaked the wall and door and burst into flame. He retreated in a stumbling hurry, beating at his hair and clothes, then plunged off into the smoke.

Owing to the draft of increasing heat, the smoke lifted pouring out through the gap in the front wall. Its direction would be reversed, Reagan knew, as soon as the back wall collapsed, for the hall and stairway beyond it would act as chimney while the gap provided a perfect through-draft. The place would go fast when that happened. He scrambled to his feet.

Frank Tillander reappeared. He had located the water cooler, lifted out its five-gallon glass reservoir, and with both hands he held it upended above his head while advancing upon that flaming door. The water gurgled out and splashed over him, but the neck of the reservoir was not large, and smoldering patches still remained on his clothes. Armed with the thing, he advanced in a crouch, as if the door were a cunning adversary. He would make another attempt to break through that sheet of fire, oblivious to any consideration of creating an instant through-draft in which he himself would be caught.

Bits of burning timber peeled off the ceiling and showered on him unheeded. Part of the wagon fell off, strewing embers before him. He wavered, balancing on his high heels, the soles of his boots too thin to withstand the heat of the floor.

Reagan drew a gun. To his mind it seemed the most reasonable act in the world to pitch a shot at the reservoir. His bullet exploded it. Glass and water cascaded down, dowsing Frank and forming a puddle at his feet.

Drenched, steam rising around him from the hot floor, Frank Tillander stood stock-still, his hands remaining upraised above his head as if continuing to hold the glass reservoir. He had taken cuts from the broken glass, for some blood mingled pinkly with the water on his face.

Reagan said, "Better move, Frank! That wall—and that floor—"

Frank stiffened, moved. He spun around, right hand diping, and whipped out a pistol that spat twice before he completed his turn. It was unlike him to waste shots. A terrible urgency was driving him, had already driven him far

124

beyond the bounds of his normally cool intelligence. Nor would he ordinarily have stood outlined in full view when forcing a gun fight, his back to that blazing inferno. His were the ways of the sharpshooter who reduced risks to a minimum.

Reagan fired and Frank's pistol tipped over, hung by its trigger guard to his finger, slipping off with the fall of Frank's arm. He said, "Come out of it!"

Frank didn't spare a look down at his shattered arm, and the pain of it, if he felt it, did nothing to wipe the wild glare from his eyes. With his left hand he conjured up another pistol. This one he raised above waist level, fast to sight, and Reagan, clipping the last fraction of a second, fired again. The pistol twirled, his shot hitting the forearm lengthwise, knocking it upward, and pain then shocked Frank into falling back a step. His heel struck a burning timber, part of the wagon. He tottered. To save his balance, he took a second backward step, heavily, both arms dangling. His boots went through the charred crust of floor, and he fell into the flames and screamed.

Reagan ran forward. A kicking leg was all he could see of Frank. He got hold of it and hauled Frank from the fire. A section of floor gave way under their weight, and he had to toil over a jumble of boards and stringers to sounder flooring. He dragged Frank onward toward the gap in the front wall. The rear wall crashed. The draft reversed itself. He felt and tasted the fresh air sucked in through the gap, and he lay gasping.

Frank was a steaming bundle of rags. The soaking had helped to fireproof his body for the moment, partly, but his head and face and hands were black. He mumbled in an anguished, sobbing manner.

A minute more, lying here, didn't matter much. Reagan said to him, "We're fools, Frank, ever to think we can make it. Settle down, I mean. Wife and all that. Solid citizens. It's not for the likes of us. We're bigger fools when we fall out and fight over it. But then we never were close friends."

Frank mumbled, "Susan! Susan Harby—trapped upstairs! Burning—"

"No," Reagan said. "Carmack's got her out before now."

He lifted Frank and carried him on out through the gap, and laid him down in the street. Everybody was rushing about except a pair standing as one: Susan and Jim. A woman jumped from a box buggy and ran to where Frank lay, and knelt at his side crying. Some people gathered around.

125

Nobody paid too sharp attention to Reagan. It dawned on him that his clothes were in ruins, that his face was bruised and sooty, that he hadn't been recognized as yet. He took his eyes off Susan. Jim Carmack's luck had finally changed, then.

He moved off, away from the blazing Hi Jolly, toward the livery barn. In shadow he allowed himself to look back at Susan, then quickly at the kneeling, crying woman. Felisa Plevin would be all soft and gentle for a while, but not for long. Her hard and dominating nature would assert itself. She'd have Frank under her thumb and keep him there. Poor Frank . . .

"What're you after now?" Heckels asked, coming upon him in the livery barn.

"Liniment," Reagan said. "For my hurts."

Heckels grinned meagerly. *"Your* hurts! Frank Tillander looks in a bad way. Badly burned. And both arms—but you know about that. How come you drug him out alive?"

"I promised his woman I wouldn't kill him. You'll see about Susan Harby, um? About her getting her rights?"

"My boss will. The district sheriff. He's coming." Heckels shifted on his stick. "I sent him strong word I couldn't handle it here. When he comes I'll turn in my badge. He'll take over till he appoints another deputy. He's tough."

"Has to be, I guess," Reagan murmured. "They saving the Hi Jolly?"

"No," Heckels said. "Everybody's busy keeping the town from burning. Wind's coming up. Your horse is in the end stall."

"Give me a hand to saddle up. This arm of mine—"

"Yeah. Ride far, Reagan. Ride long. Don't come back."

At the Papago Hills fork he drew in to look at the hills outlined against the early-morning sky. That ranch, that jewel of a ranch, the Rocking H. And Susan . . .

He shook his head. "Not for the likes of us, Frank."

He nudged his horse onward down the road. He flexed the fingers of his left hand. The numbness was leaving his arm. He was getting some feeling back in it. He would be able to go on manipulating the tools of his two trades, cards and guns, wherever he went. A good thing.

If he had lost something, well, they said that you never missed what you never had. Liars. But he wouldn't dream about it, ever again. Let it go.

L(eonard) L(ondon) Foreman was born in London, England in 1901. He served in the British army during the Great War, prior to his emigration to the United States. He became an itinerant, holding a series of odd jobs in the western States as he traveled. He began his writing career by introducing his most widely known and best-loved character, Preacher Devlin, in "Noose Fodder" in *Western Aces* (12/34), a pulp magazine. Throughout the mid thirties, this character, a combination gunfighter, gambler, and philosopher, appeared regularly in *Western Aces*. Near the end of the decade, Foreman's Western stories began appearing in Street & Smith's *Western Story Magazine*, where the pay was better. Foreman's first Western novels began appearing in the 1940s, largely historical Westerns such as *Don Desperado* (1941) and *The Renegade* (1942). The *New York Herald Tribune* reviewer commented on *Don Desperado* that "admirers of the late beloved Dane Coolidge better take a look at this. It has that same all-wool-and-a-yard-wide quality." Foreman continued to write prolifically for the magazine market as long as it lasted, before specializing exclusively for the book trade with one of his finest novels, *Arrow in the Dust* (1954) which was filmed under this title the same year. Two years earlier *The Renegade* was filmed as *The Savage* (Paramount, 1952), the two are among several films based on his work. Foreman's last years were spent living in the state of Oregon. Perhaps his most popular character after Preacher Devlin was Rogue Bishop, appearing in a series of novels published by Doubleday in the 1960s. George Walsh, writing in *Twentieth Century Western Writers*, said of Foreman: "His novels have a sense of authority because he does not deal in simple characters or simple answers." In fact, most of his fiction is not centered on a confrontation between good and evil, but rather on his characters and the changes they undergo. His female characters, above all, are memorably drawn and central to his stories.